Published by Black Balloon Publishing
www.blackballoonpublishing.com

© 2013 by Robert Perisic
Translation © 2013 by Will Firth
All rights reserved

ISBN-13: 978-1-936787-05-0

Black Balloon Publishing titles are distributed to the trade by
Consortium Book Sales and Distribution
Phone: 800-283-3572 / SAN 631-760X

Library of Congress Control Number: 2012919026

Cover art by Joanna Neborsky • joannaneborsky.com
Designed and composed by Christopher D Salyers • christopherdsalyers.com
Printed in the United States of America

9 8 7 6 5 4 3 2 1

OUR MAN IN IRAQ

BY ROBERT PERISIC

TRANSLATED FROM THE CROATIAN BY WILL FIRTH

BLACK BALLOON PUBLISHING • NEW YORK

CONTENTS

DAY ONE

✉
From: Boris <boris@peg.hr>
To: Toni <toni@peg.hr>

"Iraky peepl, Iraky peepl."
That's the password.
They're supposed to answer: "I'm sorry."
"I'm sorry."
No sweat.
Yeah! What a view—endless columns on the road from Kuwait to Basra.
The 82nd Division's Humvees, armored vehicles, tankers, bulldozers.
The place is full of camouflaged Yanks and Brits, the biological and chemical carnival has begun, and me, fool that I am, I haven't got a mask. They're expecting a chemical weapons attack and say Saddam has got

tons and tons of the shit.

I dash around with my camera and ask them all to take my photo. It's not for keepsakes, I keep telling them, it's for the paper.

The columns pour along King Faisal Road toward the border. Dust is always coming from somewhere.

"Iraky peepl, Iraky peepl."

"I'm sorry."

We continue on our way.

I keep looking to see if there are any pigeons. I've heard that the British biological and chemical detection team allegedly has pigeons.

There were none in the Land Rover Defender. They set up an air analyzer there that registers the smallest changes in the composition of the air. It's a simple, soldierly device. You don't need to think: when the indicator goes red, things are critical.

That's what they say.

Things would be critical anyway, even without it.

Things are critical with me.

I see all those pieces of iron, pieces of steel, and I'm shut into a piece of metal myself. I can hardly breathe in here.

The 82nd Division's Humvees. I watch them. They don't know I'm inside.

Or do they? The British soldiers don't want to introduce themselves. They say they're not allowed to. For security reasons.

This job is fucked. I say I'm a reporter from Croatia. I tell them my name and ask if they've got pigeons.

I ask if it's true that the NBC team (short for nuclear, biological, chemical), if it's true that they've been given cages with pigeons.

No reply.

I tell them I've heard about it. Birds are apparently the best detectors of airborne toxins because they're more sensitive than humans.

Then they reply. They say they've heard the story too
but they're not sure if it's true.
They've got masks, like I said. But sometimes they take
them off and show themselves.
I don't know if they're hiding the pigeons or if they
really haven't got any.
Do what you like with this. I think the bit about the
pigeons is interesting.
A good illustration: pigeons or doves in Iraq, the
symbol of peace and all that.
I made up the bit with the passwords.

It wasn't New Year's Eve, but never mind. I entered the flat
carrying some plastic bags and called out in a deep voice from
the door: "Father Time is here!"

She held her hand coyly over her mouth.

I put the bags down next to the fridge.

"But that's not all," Father Time said, standing up tall and
proud. "I've brought some drugs too!"

I hadn't really, but never mind.

"Oooo, lucky me, lucky me," she chirped. "I can see you're
already smacked up."

"Just a bit."

"Naughty you," she said.

"That's just the way I am, Miss."

She gave me a loud kiss on the cheek.

"Hey, Miss, where were you when I was shooting up? In
Biology, learning about the birds and the bees?" I said to
remind her who's older here.

"And pneumonia," she said.

"Where does pneumonia come into it?" I asked.

But we were already laughing, breaking character. Not
that I really knew why. Part of our love thrived on nonsense.

We could talk about non-existent drugs or whatever. I guess that element of the absurd helped us relax. One of us would say something silly and the other would laugh. We enjoyed exchanging insults.

I think she started it, long ago.

Her name was Sanja. I'm Toni.

We met after the war, under interesting circumstances: I was Clint Eastwood and she the lady in the little hat who arrived by stagecoach in this dangerous city full of rednecks. I watched as she climbed out, a fag between her lips, and the smoke and sun got in my eyes. She had a whole stack of suitcases, bound to be full of cosmetics, and I saw straight away that she'd missed her film and I'd have to save her in this one.

All right, sometimes I told the story this way because I was tired of telling the truth. Our first meeting never ceased to fascinate her. Whenever she got in a romantic mood she made me tell the story again. The beginning of love can never be recaptured. That self-presentation to the other, putting yourself in the best light, striving to be special. You play the game, you believe in it, and if it catches on, you become different.

How do you tell a story if everything is full of illusions from the beginning?

I had several versions.

One went like this: She had a red strand in her hair, green eyes, and was punkishly dressed. It's the domain of bimbos with certain deviations in taste. And that's how she behaved too, not quite upright, boyish, deviant; she looked a bit wasted, a look that trendy magazines called heroin chic. I took note of her when she first came to the Lonac Café, but I didn't go up to her because her pale face revealed apathy and pronounced tiredness from the night before. You know those faces that

still radiate pubescent contempt and the influence of high
school reading lists. People like that don't want to live in a
world like this, they can't wait to cold-shoulder you when you
approach—as if that's what gives their life meaning.

At this point Sanja usually thumped me on the shoulder—
"Idiot!" she would say—but she loved it when I wrapped her in
long sentences.

"Anyway, I didn't go up to her. I just watched her out of the
corner of my eye and blew trails of smoke into the night."

She liked to listen to how I eyed her from the side. That
refreshed the scene, a bit like when the country celebrates its
independence and patriotic myths as retold through history
and official poetry ornamented with lies.

"It was in front of the Lonac Café one day: I remember her
crushing out a cigarette with a heavy boot, and then she turned
in her long, clinging dress, with a little rucksack on her back,
and looked at me with the eyes of a young leopardess. She
stalked up to me as if she'd sighted a herd of gnus."

Basically we were so cool that this crossing of paths was
almost inconsequential.

Wotcher Ned, how's them parsnips comin' along? How's
the harvest goin', cuz? Hey bro, where ya been? That's how
city kids mess around with mock swagger and rural ethos!
We had no idea if we fitted any of those roles. At home you're
someone's child and you roll your eyes; you study at uni
and you roll your eyes; then you go out into the world and
become your own film star and you roll your eyes because no
one gets your film, and you pine away unrecognized in these
backwoods of Europe.

I acted in many films before they took me for my role in
this serious life: I worked as a journalist and wrote about the
economy. She managed to become an actress with a capital "A,"
just like she always dreamed.

"How was the rehearsal?" I asked.

She waved dismissively as if she wanted to take a rest from it all.

"Is there anything in there for us?" I asked when I saw the classifieds lying open on the coffee table.

"There are a few we could call."

She read out loud about refined apartments with charm. I closed my eyes and listened to the square footage and the location of the flats, the descriptions of amenities and neighborhoods. Peaceful, quiet street, air conditioning, lift.

And soon we were climbing up into the clouds, up above that quiet street. We imagined that life, looking down at everything. But it wasn't one hundred per cent definite that we needed that peace and quiet. Or amenities like close to the tram line and schools. That made us think of our children growing up too quickly, moving from kindergarten to high school and then onto university.

Refurbished attic flat, right in the heart of the city center, with parking space.

Immediately we saw ourselves coming down from that penthouse, going from café to café with everything close by, like when you go out to get cigarettes and meet a whole load of people and breathe in the tumult of the street, with its boundless life.

We did this every day. Hovering in weightlessness and reading the listings, we felt life was light and variable, and we thoroughly understood people who added the word "urgent" after the description of the flat.

"Come on."

"You do it."

"I called last time," I said

"Give me the phone then."

It was nicer to read those descriptions in weightlessness than to descend into the lower levels of the atmosphere and talk about actual places with actual people, hear their business-like voices. There was something draining about those conversations.

Still, we had to ring that number. The one with "urgent" next to it.

We'd been in our flat for a bit too long, that was for sure, and were starting to get sick of the furniture, which the landlord had dumped there. My friend Markatović and his wife Dijana had bought an apartment on credit and furnished it futuristically: it was spacious and spacy. When we visited they cooked slow food for us, we drank Pinot Grigio from Collio Goriziano and in that light, roomy designer apartment felt part of a new elite. Each time we returned from their place our rented flat looked like a charity shop. They had boldly moved into a new world, while we dwelled among the dark wardrobes of aunts long dead.

We didn't talk about that openly, but I sensed the disappointment in the air. I even found myself wondering if I was successful in life. I mean, what sort of question is that? I'd only just begun to live after the war and all that shit. I'd only just caught my breath again.

But there we were, one time when we'd returned from Markatović's and that fatal organic food. It was heavy in my stomach and I couldn't sleep, so I got a beer out of the fridge and looked around at the cramped ugly flat. Why don't you take out a loan too, whispered a bewildering voice. Just look at Markatović, the voice said, he's your generation, and he's got such a fancy place, and even twins. Why couldn't you have that too?

Hmm, me and a loan, a loan and me.

At my age, my old man tells me every time, he'd already . . . . And at my age my ma had already . . . . What can I say when

I think how they lived back then? They didn't have enough money to buy shoes, but they still had children and even built a house. So, naturally, they wonder what Sanja and I are thinking. I looked at our Bob Marley poster on the wall. What does a Rasta think? But he just holds his joint enigmatically between his lips. We have Mapplethorpe's black male torso on the other wall, which motivates me to do sit-ups regularly. That's what we've invested in.

When I slept here the first time, Sanja's rented flat seemed quite chic: situated on the fifteenth story of a tower block, above a tram loop. Standing by the window, the view was so good that I was afraid of falling out of it.

Of course, we came back drunk that first night. We were careful not to be loud because of her flatmate. I couldn't come. She tried to give me a blow job. It was nice that she tried, although her teeth scratched. We kept on screwing; the condoms dried out quickly and kept bunching up around the head of my dick. I finally came in the third round.

I dropped by again the next day, but skipped it on the third day so it wouldn't look like I'd moved in. I tried to stick to some kind of rhythm, so my moving in was never officially confirmed. I'd visit in the evenings, spontaneously, as if I'd heard there was a good film on TV. I haven't organized anything and I don't have any expectations, I wrote to her on a postcard that I sent from Zagreb to Zagreb just for fun. She liked that. She liked everything I said.

At breakfast I made jokes, as fresh as morning rolls, and also entertained her flatmate. It wasn't hard to make Ela laugh, and it seemed she didn't object to a guy hanging around the house in undies. So she slept in the bedroom, while Sanja and I curled up on the couch in the living room. When we made love we'd lock the door with a quick, quiet turn of the key. Later we'd quietly unlock it and run to the bathroom.

For the first year I kept on paying rent for my basement bedsit in another part of the city so as not to lose my independence. My things were there, I'd say. When I went there I'd lie on my back, all independent, listen to my old radio and stare at the ceiling.

Once Ela found a little pile of my laundry in the washing machine and said with a look of mild disgust, "Aha, so you two are in a serious relationship then."

I said to Ela by way of apology, "I haven't got a machine, you know."

They both began to laugh. They laughed long and hard.

"He hasn't got a machine," they repeated, started giggling again, and were soon hooting with laughter.

But Ela soon found herself a new flat.

Our sex became louder. The ladies down in the shop started calling me "neighbor."

It all ran by itself, without any particular plan. We enjoyed that experiment. We went on our first summer holiday together, then there were autumn walks in Venice, the Biennale, Red Hot Chili Peppers in Vienna, Nick Cave in Ljubljana, a second summer holiday, a third, Egypt, Istria, and so on. Mutual friends, parties, organizing things. Everything rolled along nicely as if nature were doing the thinking for us.

Now and then I asked myself: What now?

Now she was calling about flats. She was trying hard to make a serious impression.

"Yes, I know where the Savica market is. Yes, I know we

need to come and look at it, but could you please tell me the price?"

She just wanted to finish the conversation.

"We'll probably drop in. I'll have to see when my boyfriend gets back from work."

"Say 'husband.'"

"What?" she cocked her head as she put down the receiver.

"Why did you lie that I was at work? Do you think it makes us sound more serious?"

"I don't know."

"If you're going to lie, say 'my husband's at work.'"

✉

From: Boris <boris@peg.hr>
To: Toni <toni@peg.hr>

Baghdad is burning, the Allied bombing has begun, yoo-hoo!
You saw it, and what can I tell you, the Allied bombing tore us out of our depression, life has become sportive, dynamic, everyone is fighting to get a word in, everything is in motion.
The Allied bombing, like when you pour sugar into coffee, night and white crystals, attractive images you see again and again. I watch the Allied bombing from the Sheraton Hotel in Kuwait City and am looking for a way to attach myself to the troops, to be embedded, but for some reason they don't trust me, which doesn't surprise me. I don't trust myself. They can probably see it in my eyes: I emit it like radiation or it comes out of me like bad breath.
I hear the alarm sirens, in Kuwait City they take them seriously, you know how it is at the beginning: people call their families, all the lines are busy, suddenly

everyone hurries home, and the traffic jams cuz, long
lines of waiting cars, and all in big cars, everyone
honks their horns from inside, out from everyone's
metal box, the windows are rolled right up, everyone is
afraid of poisonous gas, people just breathe the air in
their vehicles, they sweat and stare out like fish, and I
don't know what to do with myself, so I go out roaming
in the gloaming in that city of tall, shining towers by
the light of the silvery moon.

OK, it's not silver, but never mind.

Everything here now depends on which country you're
from, and Croatia's decided to be against the war,
so Lieutenant Jack Finnegan, the officer liaison with
journalists, doesn't believe me when I say I'm on their
side, he won't give me a press ID card because in his
eyes I represent Croatia. So I go out walking around
Kuwait City in the name of Croatia; I look at the shop
windows in the name of Croatia. They say several
missiles came down in the sea, and the government
has closed the schools for seven days.

On TV kids yell in the streets, they party in front of the
American embassy somewhere in Europe, I see them
as they enter the public eye, they present themselves,
everyone has a chance to be someone as long as the
Allied bombing lasts. Gravity increases, everything
gains weight, your voice gains character, and character
means enjoyment.

Otherwise I guess I've become punked in Kuwait
City—I've lost weight and developed dark circles under
my eyes. Do you remember the first sirens? You think
something's going to happen up there, right at that
moment, things will be resolved, you think it'll soon be
over and last no longer than a war film. But it turns
out more like a boring TV show. You dash down to the
shelter, stand around until the episode's over, later
you run there a second time, and wait for it to happen.
Here people rushed to the shelters three times today,
nothing's happened and they're crazy already.

I read these emails on my laptop and kept things to myself. Sanja concluded another conversation and hung up the phone.

"Renovated attic, in the city center, 55 square meters. Now he mentioned there are sloping walls. I don't know, we have to see it. I told him we'd come tomorrow."

"Tomorrow is your dress rehearsal," I reminded her.

"I have a break, and it'll do me good to get out and stretch my legs."

"OK," I said.

In those days, guys who cook were coming into fashion so I bought a book by an English cook who had his own television show. I opened it on the counter as if I was about to chop it up. I read and leafed through the pages with knife in hand: so many recipes, so much food. I put down the knife because I'd decided to make spaghetti.

But, all the same, I kept muttering in a nasal-twanged English while I spun around the kitchen. "Itts veri fasst. Veri fasst. Naw wee edd sum beens."

The spoken instructions didn't match the cooking of spaghetti carbonara but helped create atmosphere.

"Itts not big filosofi. Poteitous, poteitou chipps. Itts simpl, itts fantastik."

I left a mess wherever I went.

"It's a disaster," Sanja said through a laugh.

She joined me and made light work where I'd been clumsy; then I hovered around her like an overeager apprentice. Although she took over everything, I kept playing the part of the guy who was cooking. I liked it when we were a good team, when we supported each other, regardless of the reality.

"I bumped into Ela today," I said.

She looked at me quizzically. "Really," she said, forking spaghetti into her mouth.

"Nothing special," I continued, "she just asked how you are."

"Actually, I rang Ela today."

"Really? Why did you ask me then?"

"I didn't ask you anything."

"Didn't you?" I said, taking some more spag.

"No, I didn't."

"Want any more?"

"No. I invited her to the premiere. She was very happy."

"Sure, you have to invite your old friend."

"How does she look? I haven't seen her since I don't know when."

Ela had been through periods of depression in recent years, and Sanja told me, after I swore secrecy, that she'd also been having clinical treatment.

"Was she fat?" Sanja asked.

"She hasn't lost weight."

"It's a disaster," Sanja sighed. "First she punishes herself with diets, then she screws someone and falls unhappily in love, then she binge eats again and ends up getting depressed."

I don't know why we became such Ela experts. We weren't actually in touch with her anymore. But we often talked about people that way; we harmonized our opinions and felt we were an organized entity.

Sanja turned her focus to the TV, which was on with the volume down low. I looked too: it was an afternoon talk show with a whole battery of columnists from women's magazines.

"Look, look, turn it up!" I said. "Icho Kamera!"

Icho Kamera, with his rugged Balkan face, his dark moustache and grizzled sideburns, was in the audience, holding the microphone and asking a question. The popular host blinked charmingly as if wondering whether she'd missed a joke. The columnists were all looking at one another.

"The remote, Sanja, the remote!"

"Over there somewhere," Sanja said.

By the time I climbed over the couch and found it, Icho had already sat down.

"Stone the squids!" I said, dropping back into the couch.

"Do you know him from back home?"

"Haven't I told you about him?"

"No, I just thought you might know him from down there because you switched to dialect straight away."

I hadn't thought about that. I was just trying to make her laugh.

As kids we used to run after him when he came to our village. We'd shout: "Icho Icho Icho!"

Our father would mutter, "Fools rush in."

At Hajduk football matches he'd stand in an empty section of the grandstand so the camera would catch him for a moment, and then he'd wave. All the cameramen knew Icho Kamera; people said they were sick of him and insiders claimed he paid them to film him. He was a well-to-do farmer who grew lettuce on an industrial scale but always went around wearing the same somber old jumper and jacket, so people didn't know if he was a miser or spent all his money traveling around after the cameras and bribing low-level media personnel. Football matches were his specialty because from there, doing a deal with the cameraman, he was best able to make it through to a mass audience.

But Icho Kamera didn't pick and choose; if he was caught in a traffic jam after a car accident he'd immediately set off for the scene of the accident and hassle the photographer. The local media's crime news archives contain a vast number of photographs of Icho Kamera who, seemingly by chance, is at the edge of the image showing a mangled Lada and a Peugeot, or we see him walking in front of a foreign exchange office that had been robbed by two masked attackers, probable drug addicts, who stormed it in broad daylight, threatening the teller with a pistol, roaring: *Take all the money out of the safe and hand it over!* Icho would just happen to be passing by. As a village child that's how I imagined turbulent city life.

Icho Kamera evoked certain emotions in me; after all, he was my first link to the outside world. Whether downhearted as he left the stadium after the team had been knocked out of the UEFA Cup qualifying round or sharing his opinion on German unification with a chance passerby, Icho Kamera from the neighboring village was an anonymous citizen of the globally mediatized world.

Later, when I planned to become an artist and developed an ironic distance to everything—and I mean everything—I intended to do some kind of "project" with Icho Kamera, the unsung hero of media culture. I enlisted my younger sister to cut out newspaper photographs of all Icho Kamera's appearances, a task she accepted willingly. My mother caught wind and of it and gave me a ferocious talking-to and explicitly forbade my sister from being involved, as if this was all something fiendish. Only afterward, as I wondered what to do with the project material we'd managed to amass, did I think of asking Icho Kamera to show me his archive; he was bound to have it all documented.

The summer the war began I once saw him from the bus; he was coming out of a shop. I got out at the next stop, rushed to catch up with him, and introduced myself, but Icho Kamera just gave me a sullen look and continued on, as haughtily as a real star. I stopped for a moment before setting off after

him, like an undaunted paparazzo, to explain the project
to him. I was going on about how what he did was a great
deconstruction of the system when he stopped short, turned,
and said, "Hop it or my boot's gonna fin' an ass to kick!"

I watched him go. He wasn't likeable at all, I realized, more
like the symptom of a disease—one I dimly understood.

That encounter dampened my enthusiasm for the project,
one of the many I didn't finish. The war had begun and
numerous chance passersby were dying, becoming media
heroes of the day, as it were, until there were too many of
them. I stopped following the soccer matches and reading
the regional papers so I hadn't seen Icho Kamera for quite
some time—until he appeared on the afternoon talk show.
He'd obviously come to Zagreb by train to be in the audience,
and then managed to get hold of the microphone to ask his
unintelligible question.

And then, at the end of the program, the camera panned over
the audience and Icho Kamera managed to fire off a last wave.

I'd dozed off a bit, and when I opened my eyes I saw Sanja
from behind, standing in front of the mirror, singing her own
interpretation of Brecht in a hushed, hoarse voice, playing a
non-existent guitar.

> *Once, in the flower of my youth,*
> *I thought I was a special bloom,*
> *Not like every farmer's daughter,*
> *With my looks and talents,*
> *My aspiring for something higher.*

When she noticed me watching she smiled bashfully.
"Hi cutie," I said softly, like a pedophile.

"I don't want to be a cutie. I'm supposed to look brassy."

"Sorry, wasn't with you."

"I have to go now."

"Already?"

"Tonight we're rehearsing the whole play for the first time."

For the last two months she'd been working on *Daughter Courage and Her Children*. Her first leading role in a major theater. The East German director Ingo Grinschgl was doing a kind of free rendering of Brecht. Sanja was Daughter Courage, and her Children were the band she performed with near the front lines. The piece was set during the Thirty Years' War. It had time-warped from the seventeenth century into the twenty-first. Things were a bit jumbled, as they often are with avant-gardists.

Daughter Courage was the band's lead singer. All the band wanted to do was live and play; a certain Council organized their concerts and saw to the overall image of the army and the war. *Daughter Courage and Her Children* was set on the Eastern Front and their enemies didn't like rock music or the West, so it looked like the band played a particular role in the clash of cultures. Impressions like this were required in higher spheres, in which the Council operated. The Children had no idea about all this, of course, and the band performed in harsh environments in front of the troops, although the majority of the soldiers would have preferred to listen to cheerful music or sentimental songs rather than their punk rock. Over time the band adapted itself to the audience and began to perform the songs they requested. Daughter Courage went along with it all just to keep the band together, since some of the band members wanted to join the army and get a taste of real fighting. She tried to get them to stay, even using sex, but the band fell apart, and in the end she remained alone with the drummer. At the end of the play she had to bare her breasts to a furious drum roll. And then everything drowned in darkness.

Ingo chose Sanja at an audition during which the candidates had to bare their boobs at the end, and prominent actresses boycotted this indignity. Only a handful of unestablished actresses and a few female exhibitionists turned up. So it was that Sanja received her first lead role, and from the very beginning there were witty comments that this was the only role officially given on account of an actress's breasts. Sanja knew she'd have to act brilliantly to counteract that humor, otherwise her career would start off on the wrong foot in this small country.

"It will all be fine tonight," I told her as she prepared to leave for the dress rehearsal.

"Jerman and Doc and their horsing around—we've wasted so much time."

Ingo didn't speak Croatian, so Jerman and Doc were slack from the beginning with learning their lines. They goofed around at rehearsals and played Brecht in a rendition of their own. Ingo was convinced he was working with real professionals. But Jerman and Doc had both recently suffered marital shipwreck. Nursing their wounds, they spent whole nights on the River Sava, dancing on a raft that had been declared a disco, and they came to rehearsals wasted. Somehow they managed the physical part of the acting, but they had no energy left for their lines.

Things went on like this for a while until Jerman and Doc let things slide just a bit too far and started slipping in modern slang, like "debacle," "no-brainer," and "aspirin"; Ingo probably just twigged to the word "aspirin" and started following the script. Although he didn't know a single word of Croatian, he quickly realized something was amiss. From then on, he came to rehearsal with an assistant to check the spoken text.

Ingo had lost faith in all of them, Sanja said. He'd become paranoid and considered her part of the conspiracy. He was growing a beard and had declared a dictatorship.

"It's a disaster."

"You do your bit and everything'll be OK. Doc and Jerman are mental, but when the panic hits them they'll get down to work."

I knew them well from my student days.

✉

From: Boris <boris@peg.hr>
To: Toni <toni@peg.hr>

Private Jason Maple removes his mask. He's 20 years old and says he's happy the war has finally started. Everyone who's squatted around in a dusty trench for months can hardly wait for something to happen. It's normal, since they've come here, otherwise nothing makes any sense, and sense is the most important thing. Even in war. It's incredibly important. Sense. You have to grasp for every scrap of sense, you just have to, for every propaganda of sense, for every lie of sense. When there's no sense, you go round the bend, madness comes out of your ears, so you have to believe in sense, particularly in war, you have to believe in sense fervently, and even after the war you have to believe with the faith of a fanatic if you want it to make any sense, otherwise it doesn't.
Jason Maple, 20 years old—I watch as the dust whirls up around him, but all that has fuckin' sense, everything is infused with the power of sense. It's the worst—nothing is crazier than sense and the wish to be imbued with it.
You need strong nerves, I say to Jason, I've got some experience, war has begun, and war is boring, boring, you have no idea how boring it can be, it's never as concentrated as it is in a film, here you're constantly on hold, and then when it happens you whack your

helmet on and you can't see, you can't see even when you're hit, you can't see it at all. When it was all over I looked at my wound, it was under my arm, and when I raised my arm it opened up, that was it, the most interesting sight of the war. War is boring, it's so boring that it drives you to other things, to the fun of war, to all those things you didn't think of doing, not in your wildest dreams, but now you want to, it'll make you become someone else, and that someone else will make sense, you'll know that it's not you, that you're not the one who enjoys it, but, in real terms, you will be the one, and you'll be a no-one when it starts to be fun, and then ask me: Where were you and what did you do?

Jason Maple is happy, he says, because it's started, and that happiness is an incredible thing: you're dirty, exposed to diseases, the air is full of hot lead, you have to salute idiots, a whole pyramid of idiots sitting on your shoulders, but you're happy. OK, you're not happy all the time, you're temporarily happy, but that too is incredible.

I was so happy when we were cleansing villages. And now I'm unhappy when I leave the flat, and I go back to check I haven't left anything switched on, so nothing catches fire, because I don't trust myself and I know what it's like when there's a fire.

I was happy when we were cleansing those villages, and that's why I don't trust myself. Today when someone talks about it, you wouldn't believe what stories there are, today when they just tell me how it was—they just need to mention it—I get unhappy, madly unhappy, aggressively unhappy. It's enough for me just to remember why I was happy back then, and I'm unhappy now, and that's why I don't trust myself. I don't trust myself, and being like that I've come to see you guys, to see your happiness, I tell Jason.

He didn't understand me at all.

I read those pieces again, they got under my skin and made me feel strangely uncomfortable; I tried to relax my shoulders and kept stretching my arms. My joints cracked. Fortunately I was interrupted by a call.

"Excuse me, did you put in the advert: Former rebel, tall and swarthy, needs a guarantor for a loan?"

It was Markatović.

"OK, former goth," I replied, "I'll remember you're interested."

"Listen, have you got time for coffee?"

"You drink too much of the stuff."

Markatović was always asking me to go for coffee, and always with a business motive. He wasn't one of those guys who vanishes when they have kids. With him it was the opposite. He had a registered firm for marketing, publishing, and all sorts of things, and he drank too much coffee all over town; he handled a million pieces of information from all sorts of different departments. He liked to say he knew half the country, and he presented himself as a link to everything.

"Come on please, I need your help—it's important."

I hadn't been to the Churchill Bar before. It was a posh place by any standards: full of fancy leather armchairs and little glass cases loaded with fat cigars. Markatović greeted me with outstretched arms as if I was just the man they had been waiting for.

Here, unhoped-for, I saw the notorious sheriff of a small town in a valley, surrounded by several bodyguards. I'd never seen the fellows before but I could tell straight away that they were bodyguards because of the way they glanced around like children looking out of a car. They were redundant, of course, because this tycoon, who went by the nickname Dolina, was himself an intimidating hulk; clearly he only kept bodyguards so as to make an even worse impression.

I had no idea what they were talking about, but straight away Markatović said that I was a genius at those sorts of things. He introduced me as an editor of the weekly *Objective* and an image specialist, and languid Dolina sized me up suspiciously.

"What's this all about?" I asked.

"A new image," Markatović answered with an air of importance. For some reason my presence made the bodyguards twitch; now they kept a cautious eye on me as if looking to see if I'd brought the new image along.

After a dramatic pause, Markatović explained to me what I already knew: this gentleman with millions of euros to his name had recently left his party, which was generally inclined toward the heavy hitters and had allowed him to amass wealth and take over his valley during the war. Markatović was therefore trying to persuade him that, without the backing of the party, he could no longer keep the same old image.

"He's in new circumstances now, politically speaking, and can't use the old image anymore," Markatović told me, although his words were intended more for Dolina.

"Yes, yes, he needs a new image," I said gruffly.

I helped out Markatović now and then. War and capitalism in the '90s had been a nasty shock to my system, and penury made me develop the habit of taking on any work, even if that meant doing three or four jobs at the same time. I actually wanted to slow down a bit now. I tried to explain to Markatović that panic was on the decline these days, but he claimed the situation now was even worse. Besides, business meant growth: you had to pay off old loans with new ones—if you didn't rush forward, the masses would catch up with you from behind. As soon as you stood still you were done for. That was Markatović's motto.

"That means the new image needs to be tailored to suit the

new situation," Markatović said to me, actually speaking to Dolina.

"That's right, the new situation," I mumbled. "Redesign is fundamental."

Dolina nodded after some difficult thinking. "Y'mean you can take care of that?"

Markatović glanced at me. But Dolina was still looking at Markatović. I suppose I wasn't making much of an impression.

It had been easy for the former goth to switch into career mode: black polo shirt, black suit, black coat, shiny black shoes. For me, an ordinary old rebel, there was no painless transition. I tried the bright, bold, and stylish. I even bought woolen jumpers, only to take off all that stuff a minute before leaving and put on my standard gear: T-shirt, leather jacket, sneakers or boots, jeans.

Markatović now explained that, with my help, he was planning to profile Dolina as a dissident who'd clashed with the powers-that-be in the capital; now he was a regionalist. Only, Dolina's valley wasn't the size of a region.

"I think he should be a microregionalist," Markatović said. "How does that sound?"

"Not quite right," I said.

"Minor detail," Markatović continued. "The task is to cast him as a dissident, a regionalist, an individualist. That's the logical conclusion since he left the party. And a liberal."

Dolina's comment? He had to go to the bathroom, so off he went, accompanied by his bodyguards.

If there were no real liberals in those backwoods we had to invent them, Markatović told me. This meant we were onto something big, because if we presented him as a liberal maybe someone sensible would join him.

"I get you," I said, "but count me out."

"All right, but just stay for a bit longer, please."

Dolina lumbered back from the toilet and sat down, breathing heavily. He looked like a good-natured alligator, smiling at me as if he were looking at a newborn baby. He hadn't just had a snort, had he?

"We've got work to do," he creaked in his thick southern dialect, patting us on the backs. "I got the councillors to walk out with me. Nice political crisis, y'know, and then elections and all that. Microregional elections. Ha, ha. Fuckin' elections."

His bodyguards smiled too.

"Just get the advert done for me and we'll move on from there," he said to Markatović. "You'll have the money tomorrow."

"Don't do that to me anymore!" I growled at Markatović when they'd gone.

"Hey, I'll devise the campaign for him in half an hour," he said. "I can't be the owner of the firm, line up the job, and then do it myself too. That'd look dilettantish. I have to bring someone else in so he sees that I've got workers."

"Thanks a million. I'd downright forgotten that I belong to the working class."

"I've worked out everything already. I just need to hire someone to do the design."

"The designer is a worker, and you'll need a photographer too—he's also a worker."

"If you want, you could travel down south and tour the area. We can pay for all that. I don't have the time. Besides, it's better that someone else goes so they think a whole team is involved."

Markatović's mobile phone rang. It was his wife, Dijana, and he told her that he was negotiating things with me— business matters. He tried to sound soothing as if he was rocking her on waves of optimism. Suddenly he looked at the mobile in surprise.

"I think she hung up on me. I'm going to the can."

He was there for a while, and when he came back he spoke softly. "Want some coke?"

There hadn't been any coke in our circles until recently. But now, it seemed, we were making progress, and the whole country was under development. It could be a treat for Sanja and her mob after the premiere and I could show off. He handed me a packet under the table and I stuck it in my pocket.

"How long have you been into that for?" I asked.

"Just recently, when the atmosphere's right."

I looked around. Not exactly what you'd call atmosphere.

Markatović leaned toward me. I could write a guide for stock-market beginners for his publishing house, he said—he knew I played around with shares a bit. He tried to persuade me; he said we lacked a reference book in Croatia because people still had socialism in their heads.

"I'll think it over."

A waitress, young and wasp-waisted, came up to the table. I ordered a beer. Markatović ordered coffee, then abruptly changed his order to a beer, and whiskey.

His face was puffy. He'd developed a beer belly. I'd say he looked quite a bit older than I although we were the same age. We'd first met at uni when we'd both just left the Yugoslav People's Army, a long time ago.

We had sniffed each other out back at the entrance exam for Economics and discovered that we'd both been cajoled into that line of study, despite our inclinations toward philosophy and art. To get me to enroll in Economics, my folks bribed me with a Sony hi-fi, a state-of-the-art system back then with a double cassette deck, and Markatović's folks bought him nothing less than a Yugo 45. But for us the most important thing was to come to the big city with all its concerts, clubs, and the vibrant social scene.

The rest of the group at the entrance exam were already discussing where they'd work after graduating. The majority were counting on government jobs, while the more avant-gardist advocated entrepreneurship and risk, which there would be more and more of in our country, they said. We sided with the pro-riskers. But we were hardly accepted into their ranks because we seemed too much of a risk. Compared with the crowd from Economics, Markatović and I looked like outright vagabonds. The crack corps of sex, drugs, and rock'n'rollists didn't make it to uni—those first rebels get bogged down early on, cannon fodder of the subculture.

Now we, in turn, advocated creative business. We pretended to admire Bill Gates and his ilk, came out with their quotes and generally sowed confusion among the straight-and-narrow Economics students. Markatović claimed to have read in *The Economist* that Gates was working on a combination of a computer and a washing machine and as such would bring a computer to every home. He was inspired by that idea throughout the 1990-91 academic year and acquired several disciples, particularly among female students.

To tell the truth, our debauched lifestyle was only accepted to a limited degree during the first semester. The nerds soon closed ranks and we were declared wastoids, especially seeing as the girls liked to sit around with us in the cellar canteen. We enjoyed that dubious reveler's reputation, and the professors' pets whispered with schadenfreude that we had no future. But somehow we managed to scrape through that academic year while the country hurtled toward war.

We were still dutiful sons and thought our elders knew where they were leading us. Then the war began in earnest. Although it'd been long brewing, it still caught us all by surprise. It was hard to muster the concentration to study. Moreover, both Markatović and I spent the end of that summer in uniform and missed the start of the third semester, but in the end we were able to present ourselves as even greater guys—heroes, almost. We enrolled for our second year on the basis of those elastic wartime documents: we had army certificates, and the lecturers didn't use us to set an example in exactitude.

During this period the world fell apart. Nothing was permanent, authorities faded and people flinched before us. We realized that we belonged to a generation that had a moral advantage because it was defending all those old folks accustomed to the molds and models of socialism. Lost as they were, they patted us on the shoulder as if they were thanking us for something. We vocally despised socialism and they agreed with us on that. We despised their life's experience and they agreed with us on that too. We disdained all they'd done and stood for, and again they agreed with us. To leave no doubt that the future belonged to us, we rejected everything that until yesterday had been of any worth. They agreed with us on all that.

Markatović now came to class wearing his camouflage jacket, and I wore mine when I needed a staff member's signature. Our self-confidence grew. We despised everyone and everything at uni. We spent most of our time in the canteen, getting blotto like big, disappointed men racked by the blues too early in life. The war went on, and in the 1991-92 academic year we were allegedly still studying Economics, down in the canteen, drinking beer and frightening the faculty with our subculture rebellion, for which the war provided an unexpected pretext. We found it amusing that no one contradicted us, although we were just ordinary assholes. Markatović would get sloshed in the canteen and then go up to people, wearing his uniform, and ask: Why does no one contradict me when I'm just an ordinary asshole? But this lifestyle led to isolation. We no longer went to lectures at all; we felt we'd lose part of our libertine integrity if we sat there like good little sons of our parents and listened to those crusty lecturers while war profiteers and politicians privatized state firms, the poor butchered the poor, concentration camps sprang up all over Bosnia, and reports came in about mass rape.

Although we never would have admitted it to each other, we were shit like the others, rickety and rotten through and through, but we wore the masks of tough lads, not knowing how else to defend ourselves. In the canteen we barricaded ourselves from the world. Besides, there were none of the concerts we'd come to the metropolis for, and the bars around the city were full of guys like us, plus the occasional real psycho.

The low-intensity war dragged on through summer, the exam season began, and students sat out on the terraces around the campus while we were still drinking down in the dark— isolated, like self-convicted felons.

We had no intention of admitting defeat. We simply con- cluded that uni was shit. We belonged elsewhere, somewhere better—we were artists, after all! No one understood us. Everyone there was counting imaginary money in advance. What were we doing among those squares and yes-men anyway? We spoke a different language. They say Croatian and Serbian are different, and back then everything was done to make them differ even more, but this gulf was incomparably greater. Our rebellion, which had built up down in the cellar, finally exploded, and we decided to go to the university registry, pick up all our documents and devote ourselves to art. I remember us rolling up there drunk, the ladies from the registry looking at us strangely, and us cheerfully going out into the sunshine with all our papers. Markatović was so exhilarated that in the parking lot he flung them into the air and we watched them flutter down on the gentle breeze.

The girls were wearing miniskirts, the war stretched out like chewing gum, and we were finally free.

Later, Markatović enrolled in first-year Literature and even published a book of poetry. The reviews said he was promising. But not a single woman fell in love with him because of his poetry, which was probably why something in him broke. His path to literary fame petered into endless procrastination, and then he met Dijana, who didn't read poetry, and they had twins, identical boys. Now he had a family to feed, so he founded his own company.

As I looked at him, puffy and bloated, a witness of my stupid biography, I realized I didn't look so great myself. After Economics I decided to switch to Drama. The competition was fierce—they were all kids from arty families, but I made it all the same.

My folks still placed all their hope in Economics, especially under the new capitalist system, and pronounced the word for Drama—*dramaturgija*—in a mystic, tragic voice, like our neighbor Ivanka back in the early '80s when she found out her son was smoking hash. The whole neighborhood heard Ivanka going round and round their yard, holding her head in her hands and moaning: "Marijuaaana. Marijuaaana. Oh my God, marijuaaana."

Under socialism, that long, undulating word was taboo; Ivanka swayed like a cobra mesmerized by a snake charmer, and that's just how my mother behaved many years later: "Draaamaturgija. Draaamatuuurgija. Oh my God, draaamatuuurgijaaa." When word got around that marijuana was a soft drug, everyone realized I'd moved on to harder stuff.

My parents, who until then had been disinterested in culture, now became its bitter enemies. When the culture program began on TV they didn't change the channel straight away anymore. Now they glowered and slighted: "Talk about

a bunch of smart asses," and "That's s'posed to feed you?" It
was hardly surprising: war had impoverished them, capitalism
had deprived them of their rights, and culture had killed off
their last hopes.

I couldn't count on their financial support, obviously,
so I started freelancing for newspapers while still studying.
I covered the infamous culture scene, dashed around all
day from one promotional event to another, where I drank
vermouth and in the evenings I'd eat canapés at exhibition
openings and premieres. That was a life full of cultural
highlights. And then, unsuspectingly, I once mentioned
in front of the editor in chief that I'd studied Economics.
The paper was full of Arts dropouts, as it turned out, and
Economics dropouts were "as rare as hen's teeth." He didn't
want to listen to my complaints, but instantly promoted me,
although many thought undeservedly, to economics editor.
I had a whole page to fill with "boring news," as the editor in
chief put it, and if I found out about any scams I was to report
them to him so they could be written up separately because
that was exclusively what he and our readers were interested
in as far as the economy was concerned. They put me on the
payroll, which saved me from my vermouth diet, but my
mother's "See, didn' we tell ya to stick to Economics?" never
failed to annoy me.

From: Boris <boris@peg.hr>
To: Toni <toni@peg.hr>

If it weren't for Jason I'd've died of boredom.
He asked me things, he said that since they'd been out
in the field they hadn't had any information, they'd

been in an information blockade for weeks, so he
asked me, What is the news?
The war's begun, man, I said, you are the news.
A long column of camouflaged bulldozers passed by.

DAY TWO

The staff entered the editorial office in dribs and drabs. I was settling into a chair, one of the better ones, reclining against the headrest. My other persona, "Mr. Journo," morphed out of nothing, master of the rational mindset. My facial muscles tensed. Wearing this mask of the salaryman demands a lot of energy. It takes your "all," as they say. And that's really the main part of the work.

The night before, after Churchill Bar, I'd been to a slew of other places with Markatović. I boast in front of women, while Markatović tends to order expensive cocktails for them. In the morning light, the salaryman differs sharply from the night owl. It's simply the pain of transformation that we call the hangover.

The editor in chief is my former friend Pero—thirty-seven years old, married, with two kids, an affair, and two loans. His problems were bigger than mine. He held his temples with the tips of his fingers and stared at his computer keyboard, silent like a father going through a difficult time.

This was an editorial meeting, nothing special, but Pero had recently been promoted so I surmised he now showed a surplus of seriousness to remind us of his new role. He'd been one of us before, but then was chosen to be launched into orbit, to a job where it's normal to call the Prime Minister's office every now and again and expect to be put through. He was still reeling a bit from the jolt. He couldn't behave like the old Pero now, and the new one hadn't yet gelled.

He wiped sweat from his brow, with difficulty, and gathered himself into what was supposed to be a whole. Chairs and rollers squeaked on the carpet. Pero took the remote and terminated the silence: the TV up in the corner of the office droned to life. Now we could see what was happening in Baghdad, where the Americans had entered a week and a half earlier. CNN talked about restoring order and electricity.

I thought, people in Baghdad have no electricity but they're constantly on television. They can't even watch themselves. And yet, at least we could during the war here. I felt that was a point worth making, but then I remembered it would be best not to mention Baghdad.

Silva and Charly came in through the glass door, both smiling. When he sat down, Charly sombered up.

"Today is one big hassle," he said.

I had a brief impulse to ask what sort of hassle, though it passed. Usually it was nothing but an everyday annoyance, something ministerial, minor, bureaucratic in nature. His complaints about life felt forced, invented solely to give the conversation weight. Charly had always wanted to have a serious chat with me, who knows why. With Silva, on the other hand, he only ever giggled.

I didn't manage to ask anything because Silva directed her unflappable, vapid coquetry at me and chirruped, "Hey Toni, your hairdo is awesome."

"Great, thanks," I said.

I received only compliments from her, which generally helped me relax, because Silva instinctively reflected the company's power dynamics in her flirting. As long as she was paying you compliments things were on an even keel, but if she told you your hair was a mess you had to think about your standing in the office.

Vladić, who there's no need to describe, looked at me from the other end of the table and said, "Yes, yes, Toni is a real himbo." He chuckled maliciously.

I started to feel uncomfortable. Was it the gel? I'd only put on a touch, what could be the problem? I made a face as if I didn't get what he was on about, and Silva kept looking at me cheerfully, with an expectant air. She was the entertainment editor, so she could always be relied on to look frivolous through even the gravest situation, even before a Session of the Supreme Soviet. She represented our lightheartedness. The rest of us, immersed precariously in the state of the nation, could summon no cheer. Our aura was tainted by the prevailing socio-political gloom, while Silva vibrated in the bright and lively colors of the boutiques she shopped in every day.

"Shall we do coffee afterward?" Charly asked me.

"No," I said. "I have to go and look at a flat with Sanja."

The Chief looked around as if he was counting his troops. We were all present. All ten of us. We sat there, aware of the conundrum our *Objective* was in—and the company in general. Today, our sister daily paper started producing losses. Or that's what the powerful *Global Euro Press*, known to us as GEP, had triumphantly published yesterday.

Our paper, which we fondly called a corporation, went

under the name of *Press Euro Global*, PEG. It'd been set up by disaffected editors who had split from GEP, and as such we weren't just a backroom club of feckless malcontents. We had a mission: to fight for truth and justice, and to hold the last line of defense against GEP's media monopoly.

The Chief muted the TV as he stood up and said, "I don't need to outline the situation for you—you've all got heads on your shoulders. We need to make a move." Taking us in with his gaze, he continued. "That's nothing new to you, right? Because what are we? We're prime movers. We make the world go round! If there were no media everything would have ground to a halt long ago. Nothing would have happened because there wouldn't have been anywhere for it to happen!"

He was putting on a dramatic performance.

"What I want to say is that nothing is going to happen by itself. Well, granted, there are things like 9/11—you can't really say that was a media-produced event."

"Some say it was," I interjected.

"Like bloody hell it was! People flew the planes up and people crashed them. But every newspaper, even the stupidest, is going to cover an attack like that, right?" He pointed to the muted television. "We can't cover what's visible, do you understand? That's what TV does, and then the dailies gnaw the bones—that's not for us!"

He'd really put some preparation into this. Months ago he used to bullshit around in the pubs. Just look what a position makes of a man! As film critics say, he's grown into his role.

"So what do we cover?"

We all looked at the Chief.

"We cover the invisible! The imperceptible!" he thundered.

This baffled me. Where did he get this theory?

"I want you to be investigative, to reflect, to come up with things! Devise and concoct story angles, show me something new. Turbo-politics was yesterday. There are no more massacres, Tudjman is dead, Milošević is finished. There's no real drama anymore. You have to turn things over. Search for new hysterias. Where's the old paranoia gone? It must still be around somewhere. It was easy in the '90s. OK, we were under attack and that wasn't easy. But the war provided information. That was our contribution to global media: we were breaking news. The world took note of us. But not anymore. Now we're ordinary. Now you have to make stories out of ordinary things. We have to shape and mold this new reality. You're all still searching for the old stories, but what's happening now is that reality is amorphous. Because you haven't shaped it yet. It's natural that our circulation is falling. That simply means: I want new creations. That's what I want. Otherwise there'll be some swift sackings."

We'd had a crisis fire-drill with every new editor. Pero, like the others, came to us as a savior. In the name of justifying the savior, ruin always has to be nigh—all religions are based on that. Permanent crisis. We can't do without ruin and the abyss. We ourselves piled high the doom-laden headlines to jolt people to life.

Young Dario responded best to the shock treatment: he was wide awake now and his eyes gleamed like a cheetah's, although he was lanky and looked more like an antelope.

After a pause the Chief said, "And then there's GEP too, as you all know."

His gaze landed on Secretary, the old status seeker, who acted the sphinx at editorial meetings.

He was no ordinary secretary, not of the clerical caste at all, in fact. He once traveled with me to Moscow, where I interviewed the oligarch Teofilakovsky because he was buying up hotels and sponsoring operas in Croatia. Wherever we went, I introduced myself as "Toni, journalist," and Russians scorned me as a busybody, but Secretary introduced himself as "the Secretary" and was accorded immediate deep respect. I still hadn't fully grasped his function, but the Russians figured him out straight away. He was a vital remnant of the old system, except that he'd shed all ideology in the cataclysmic system change.

He told me in vodka-induced elation that he'd once been a Communist, only later to try out all of the parliamentary parties. He'd finally come to rest in the Croatian Peasant Party. He discovered they were the best when he first went out to a rural event—there was real hospitality in the country. Afterward you needed at least one day of sick leave. The Peasant Party was probably a double-edged sword, he said, because since being a member his cholesterol had gone up and his gout had returned with a vengeance, like in the good old days.

"Secretary will brief someone on the GEP issue," the Chief explained.

We were constantly exposing GEP's covert attempts to monopolize the market. GEP had secret subsidiaries and false fronts. They were at us from all sides; they stole stories from us and featured them first. We suspected they had a mole among the editorial staff. In order to demoralize us, they cherry-picked our journalists with extravagant salaries. Every so often a colleague would disappear, never to be mentioned again. The PEG management responded to these dastardly attacks by preemptively burning the bridges: all PEG staff had to produce several anti-GEP pieces, engaging in heated polemics with them, calling them criminals and foreign spies, in the hopes that they'd be unable to go over to those they'd so zealously abused. We didn't need trust falls or paintball—newspaper warfare was our team building exercise.

I'd distinguished myself early in the newspaper war before appreciating the finer nuances of burning bridges. And as a result, I was attached to PEG permanently. That's how it is in small countries: the room to maneuver is abominably narrow.

Secretary held a note in his hand and looked around through his glasses.

"Any volunteers?" the Chief asked.

I saw Dario fidgeting in his chair—you could tell he was about to volunteer, but he didn't know if the others had precedence. His instincts told him it was a great honor to take on an anti-GEP topic.

I was probably like that once, too, before I caught on— around the time the current owner bought us. He was a fallen tennis player who had parlayed his fame into owning newspapers. During the war he played recreationally with the former president and let him win points, for which he was rewarded discount shares in several state firms. At that time the president personally edited the daily current-affairs program, *The Evening News*, and we reporters became official "fighters for the truth." Circulation rose. The ex tennis player was our chief shareholder. Now it was just a job.

The democratic processes brought the interest rates down.

I applied for the loan.

In the end, Dario was the lucky volunteer.

From: Boris <boris@peg.hr>
To: Toni <toni@peg.hr>

This afternoon, three Iraqi Scuds were fired at the Anglo-American convoys heading for the border. They came down one after another, twenty minutes before I arrived on the scene of the miss. Please introduce me as "Boris Gale, reporting from the scene of the miss." Usually reports come from the scene of an

event, but in war you can only report from the scene
of the miss. I mean, if it'd been a hit I wouldn't be able
to report it. That needs explaining to the readers. So:
"Here's a report from the scene of the miss from our
correspondent . . ." But listen, write what you want,
that's your job.
There were two others with me at the scene of the
miss, Italians—since I'm an impoverished reporter they
let me hop in the back of their jeep.
Like I say, we just arrived there. But they sent us back
straight away. They were all in complete NBC gear with
masks, rubber gloves, and rubber boots.
Rubber, rubber, and more rubber. That's my report.
A non-event, a miss.
Gumboots in the sand, a huge sky.
Nothing to say.
The soldiers in rubber made us skedaddle.
We zoomed off into the desert.
Ciao!

We discussed topics for the next issue. I announced an
interview with the old economist Mr. Olenić who was in the
front seat for all the economic reforms of the last decades.
    Silence.
    "He has all sorts of anecdotes," I added.
    Pero nodded.
    When the meeting had finished the Chief stopped me,
"And our man in Iraq?"
    I waited for the others to file out.
    "That boy in Iraq—is he still there?"

I'd been suppressing it for too long. It was time for an admission.
    The fellow we sent to Iraq didn't have any journalistic

experience. I'd praised him to Secretary. "Wow, what hat did you pull him out of?" he'd asked, impressed that my man knew Arabic.

"Oh, you know me," I said—I was famous for my personnel conjuring acts.

Then Secretary took the matter before Pero. That was probably the first thing the Chief gave his rubber stamp. He was itching to make decisions, and the recruitment of ambitious amateurs went together perfectly with the paper's cost-cutting policy.

The guy we sent to Iraq was called Boris, and there was a catch. Boris is a cousin of mine. I didn't tell anyone about that. I hadn't seen the need to reveal this bit of information. With Arabic Studies on his CV he was made for the job. But now I began to feel the bond of kinship. Not only had I recommended a guy who played the fool instead of writing normal reports, but it turned out that I'd fraudulently employed one of my stupid relatives. I pretended to be a suave European intellectual but in secret I was clowning around for my clan. I saw now that I was going to be caught red-handed.

I wanted to blame my mother. She gave my phone number to everyone. When you look at it, it really isn't natural: people flock to the capital like blind mice, the city grows like a tumor, and half the bloody population has my number in their pocket, including Boris. As if sending me some forgotten debt, she'd mediated before the local community as a representative of my "success" in the world. As soon as I'm out of earshot she boasts that I'm Mr. Big in Zagreb. And there you go, people hold her to her word; she's practically opened an office at home, receives petitioners and passes on my number. I then get called by people who I'd forgotten even existed. They call me about the most unlikely things, like a pension or operation, the local water supply, the anniversary of their brigade from the war, a pedophile on the beach, and when I answer the phone they invariably ask: "Guess who this is?"

They ask that to see if remember them. When I hear that, I know it's them because no one else plays that guessing game. And I start to feel like someone woken abruptly from sleep, because I'm suddenly confronted with all the forgotten sounds of my home dialect. That "guess who this is" activates a whole backlog of memories and, I must say, I very often guess correctly.

Each time I say "I'll see" and dread when they're going to call again. And they do call again, and again, until a feeling of guilt comes over me for having absconded and become such an individualist, and then I promise to do all I possibly can. Without this provincial pressure I'd obviously never have recommended cousin Boris for Iraq because I saw that he was crazy.

I mean, now it was clear to me that I'd seen it straight away, but I guess I wanted everything to be different.

Huh, that won't be easy to explain to Pero the Chief.

I stood before him now with that whole explanation in my mind.

He looked at me as if he was pondering the inscrutable. "When's he coming back?"

From: Boris <boris@peg.hr>
To: Toni <toni@peg.hr>

The Yanks took out some Brits. They downed a helicopter with their friends in it. Poor coordination. "Identify yourself, Identify yourself"—and blam! That's friendly fire for you.
But it's all logical.
We're fighting for the Iraqis, for their democracy, for

their well-being. We all love each other. Every victim is
an accident. It's all friendly fire.
Friendly fire has been around ever since the notion
of humanity has existed. Christianity too, of course,
and crusading Christianity and missionary Christianity
faced with pagan tribes, where they killed half so the
others would understand, everything is friendly. It's
only us in the Balkans who still kill each other with
hatred, without real ambitions. The rest is friendly fire.
The Brits got stroppy, but they shouldn't have. The
Yanks don't have it easy either. It's all the same: Brits,
Iraqis, civilians—wherever you fire you hit a friend.
I don't know what more to say about that.

It turned out that Sanja couldn't go and see the flat.

I sat down to have a coffee with Charly and now he was
telling me about a woman he'd screwed because he was
smashed.

With his receding chin and wandering eye, he was less than
an Adonis, but he was tenacious: he became best friends with
the blondes he couldn't bed and tried, at least in public, to
give the impression of being a couple. He suffered from high
standards in every respect. He even made a kind of career out
of it, writing gastronomic columns: recommended the most
expensive wines, reviewed restaurants, created a sophisticated
image in the midst of our post-revolution hangover, while
driving around in his fat Jag. Charly always knew what was
trendy and what you weren't allowed to ridicule: sailing,
diving, and head hunters had recently enjoyed immunity, as
well as Asian films, gardening, and slow food.

"But man, when the morning light filtered in through the
blinds," Charly described the horrific moment. "And now the
woman keeps calling me and wants to go out for coffee. The

craziest thing is that I splurged on her. We drank probably twenty cocktails and I overdrafted my account."

I looked around, waiting for this to blow over.

But the truth is the truth, she's a good shag, www dot perversion dot com. You know her, in fact."

"What's her name?"

"Ela."

"Fuck, man, you really are an asshole."

Charly laughed and nodded with a cheesy grin.

"Just look at him!" I said, glancing around as if addressing a jury. "What's so damn funny? She's a friend of my girlfriend's."

"Take it easy. She's not your girlfriend."

"She's not ugly. If she lost a few kilos she'd be cool."

"Sure she's OK, I never claimed otherwise," he defended himself. "What are you getting so hung up about?"

I intentionally didn't fall silent when Silva sat down. She was one of those blondes; she gave up modelling, with an extramarital baby in arms, and joined the editorial staff thanks to Charly.

Charly pretended to be searching for something in the pile of newspapers he'd brought with him.

"I know her pretty well."

"Hey, have you seen this?" Charly exclaimed, trying to change the topic. "In Solin near Split there are eight betting shops in a thirty-meter radius."

Silva nodded.

He opened the newspaper. "A guy says: 'You oughta come Sundays after Mass, that's when it's busiest.'"

"Who were you talking about just now?" Silva asked.

"A girl from accounting," Charly lied. "She messed up a payment to me. Claimed she's a birdbrain, but Toni defends her."

"Why are you standing up for her?" Silva asked me.

Charly scowled at me.

"The girl's OK," I said to Silva.

"From Accounts? Seriously? Is this something new?"

I had no idea now what she was thinking. Should I conceal what we were talking about, or tell her I was fucking my way through Accounts?

"What's wrong with the girls on the editorial staff?" she asked.

"I mean: en masse from Mass to the betting shop." Charly fought for attention. "That beats them all. Where else do you have anything like that?"

"Most people go to church to improve their chances," Silva said.

Charly rolled with laughter. You could see he considered her the wittiest person in Europe.

"May I sit here?" our youngest colleague Dario asked.

He kept popping up at our table ever more frequently. He probably saw mixing with us as a way of moving up in the world.

"Yes, yes," I said, looking up gratefully—he'd come at just the right time to kill that conversation.

Dario sat down and whispered, "Whaddaya think? Didya hear the Chief?" He turned toward me, seeking an ally. "By the way, I think those reports from Iraq are fantastic."

"It's a standard piece, but there's a lot of work in it."

"I don't know, I've had enough of wars," Silva joined in.

Me too, I said to myself.

From: Boris <boris@peg.hr>
To: Toni <toni@peg.hr>

Saddam is a young villager from the outskirts of
Basra. He was named after the president. What can
he do? He spreads his hands, spreads his hands wide
like a scarecrow, and I spread mine too, spread mine
wide, and we chat like two scarecrows in the field,
except there are no crops, no plants, no grass, and no
birds for us to scare away, only sand and scrap iron.
His village, said Saddam, is in a bad place, a very bad
place. There's fire there, he says, a lot of fire, so he
stuck all his goats in a pickup truck and took to the
road like Kerouac, except there's no literature, no
Neal Cassady, no poetry, no shade under the vine, as
they say back home. His tire burst, and Saddam the
goatherder was out on the Basra-Baghdad highway,
with a flat tire and there was no spare. So Saddam is
patching his tire, the goats are bleating in the pickup,
an idyllic scene. Abrams tanks pass by, all looking
ahead, amassed forces around Saddam's goats.
I crouch beside him, looking at the tire, as if I'm going
to help, but I don't.

When he started to send me his psychedelics, I called him by
satellite phone. He acted as if he didn't hear me well, a bad
connection. Since then he hadn't been in touch by phone. He
wrote that it's dangerous, they can be located, but he continued
to send emails every day.

Then I cursed at him in an email, telling him to come back.
No answer.

I parked near our apartment block in front of the Last
Minute Travel Agency. In the window big letters advertised

THAILAND, NEW YORK, CUBA, TIBET, MALAGA, KENYA. Every day you could decide at the last minute.

Would I go to Cuba? Or to New York—the center of the universe? Or to Tibet, to have a revelation and come back a new person?

That wouldn't be bad, I thought.

I saw straight away how he looked at me when we met a month ago in Zagreb after years of not seeing each other.

The layout guy Zlatko had had a baby daughter that day and treated us to a round of drinks; afterward I went and sat in the bar close to the office to wait for Boris. Cuz was over half an hour late.

I expected he'd got lost. But then I saw him coming along the street, glancing around cautiously. His gait took me back to when we were teenagers and greeted each other loudly with a clap on the shoulder and a yell of "Hey, old chum." We learned a rakish swagger: walking broad-legged with our hands in our pockets as it if was cold. We put on a show of enthusiasm when we met in bars and clubs because we were relying on each other in the event of a fight, I guess.

He was wearing orange-tinted shades and smiled like a mafioso pretending to be a Buddhist. Sinewy, with a longish face, we'd always been similar. He even had a streak of color in his hair, a yellowish stripe behind his ear. He looked quite urbane. You could tell he didn't live in our village, which incidentally has expanded quite a bit but still isn't a city, so we called it a "settlement."

But Boris lived in Split—cuz was a city boy, good on him. I wouldn't need to feel embarrassed if anyone I knew passed by.

He acted so sluggishly that I thought he was smacked out. But he said he'd been clean for a long time. Now he told me he'd come to the big smoke because, like, there's no perspective back 'ome. He wore his underdoggery in a slightly high-handed way like victims of the system do. Soon he took out some sheets of paper and handed them to me.

The pages were densely typed with a worn ribbon—you could hardly see the words, but I made them out best I could as he just stared straight ahead, smiling at the fruit juice he'd ordered, smoking Ronhills and blithely blowing rings.

He'd given me poems in prose on some intangible topic. Never mind, I thought, at least he was literate, and that was something.

"You need to take this to a literary magazine and let them have a look," I said.

"It doesn't matter. I can do any kind of writing." He started tapping with his leg. His smile faded.

"Look, this is literature of sorts, it's special in its own right. For newspapers you need to write concisely."

"That's even easier."

"If there's an opening, I'll let you know."

"Fine," he said, as if I was abandoning him.

When he asked me what my girlfriend did I felt like I was boasting.

Once, long ago, we listened to the same records and were so alike in dress and behavior that old grandma Lucija could hardly tell us apart; and now look at us. I recognized myself in him but watching him now I seemed to remind him of some form of injustice. He looked at me like an apparition that had been magically beamed from the summertime shallows where we played "keepy-uppy" in our swimming trunks, into the actors' jet set, and from there had skydived down into a newspaper office overflowing with cash.

"I could write what no one else will," Boris said "It's no sweat for me."

"Shall we have another drink?"

"I've only got 20 kunas."

"It's on me."

I ordered another beer and he—I couldn't believe it—another juice. The conversation wasn't going to get more fluid.

"Don't you drink?" I asked.

"Now and then."

I launched into a spiel about my drinking habits—an inane, incoherent story. But I had to say something so we wouldn't sit there like two logs. We sat there for a little longer and finally he mentioned his degree, which he hadn't been able to finish.

"Sorry, what was it that you studied again? I just remember it was pretty exotic."

"Arabic."

"Iraq," I said, thinking, thinking. Rabar, the only true go-getter on the staff, had defected to GEP a month earlier, and now he was reporting for the competitors in Kuwait. Here was a job in the offing.

"Morocco," he said sadly.

"What about Morocco?"

"Dad was chief engineer; we had servants and a pool. Then—wham!—the old man had a heart attack. Right there by the pool."

"Yes. I know."

He'd gone to the international school, but they also learned Arabic. Every time he thought of something in Arabic he'd remember his old man. Once he'd overheard two Arabs talking in the street; he followed them to a café, sat at the next table, and listened to them. He understood everything they said. After that he enrolled in Arabic in Sarajevo but couldn't finish uni because the war began.

"OK, and now have a think about this," I said. "Would you go to Iraq? The Yanks are going to attack any day."

"Sure!"

"Now, our guy who went to war zones had his ways of doing things. I don't know how, but he always coped. He sent things by mail—the photos and the texts. There are also these satellite phones."

"No probs, I'll get the hang of it."

"Have a good think. It's war."

"No sweat."

"Sure?"

"Peace has become a problem for me."

He'd been there for a month.

When Sanja entered the apartment I was pretending to read a Jimi Hendrix biography. I must have looked even more dejected than I felt.

"Are you angry? Listen, I really couldn't go and see the flat," she said straight away. "I ran into a journalist from *The Daily News*."

"You're joking, from GEP? How long did you talk for?"

"An hour maybe. Plus the photo shoot."

"That's more than a little statement. Was it a proper interview?"

"Don't worry, I was careful not to let any cats out of the bag," she smiled, noticing the remnants of the pizza on the table.

"I've already eaten, I couldn't wait," I said.

"No trouble. We ordered a whole pile of kebabs. Do I stink?" She imitated a naughty child and fumigated me with her onion breath, trying to kiss me while I kept trying to evade her.

In the end I let her kiss me, but then it wasn't fun for her anymore.

OUR MAN IN IRAQ   51

"Have Jerman and Doc been cramming their lines?"

"Ingo has moved the dress rehearsal to eleven in the evening. He has to work with them before that. But the craziest thing is he gives me more shit than he does to any of the others. I mean, they disrupt me too, but he comes down on me to assert his authority."

"Well well, the progressive vents his fury on the girls!"

"All he tells me is that I have to act like a punk. His spiel is, like, I have to rebel against how others see that role." She imitated his way of smoking while constantly looking up at the ceiling. "He shouts at me all day."

"He's obviously panicking. You all are."

"I know. But today I was about to tell him where he could stick it. If punk's what you want, punk's what you'll get."

I adored her like this: her pugnacity, her independence, her attitude.

"Well, tell him where he can shove it!" I said.

"I will!"

"He should think twice, it's too late to throw you out now!"

I wanted her to feel my support. She had to act with conviction and show she was prepared to defend herself. She wasn't going to swear at the director, but she should at least feel that she could.

Sanja was against Boris going to Iraq, against the war, against anyone writing about such a spectacle, against infotainment, and I had an inkling she wasn't exactly enthusiastic about my relatives either. OK, neither am I, but I always defended them.

I assured her that it wasn't because he was a relative of mine but because he was the right person for the job—he knew Arabic, he was literate, and war wasn't a problem for him. I'd spared her all the details but I had to talk to someone so I

gave her a quick rundown of the situation and, of course, it all
sounded like a confirmation that she was right.

"A mistake," I concluded.

"You're too sentimental. Your relatives are just using you."

"Can we talk about something else?"

"I had a kind of premonition, but you were so enthusiastic
about him."

"Who me? Enthusiastic?"

"Don't get angry. You're just a bit naive, you misjudge
people."

She waited for me to say something.

I waited too.

It was the same silence that followed us during our third
summer together when we did set off on an official tour to
meet the in-laws: several days with hers, several days with mine.

It felt a bit like an actor's workshop: we watched each other
fine-tune our performance, took care that the other didn't put
their foot in their mouth, sat at the table stiffly and respectably
and exchanged pleasantries in regional slang. I didn't exactly
know my lines. But I talked about the high price of living,
various ailments, and car accidents.

They asked us about our life in Zagreb in a well-intentioned,
worried tone and suspected we were living the wrong way; we
tried to stick to factual matters and somehow extricate ourselves
because we couldn't openly admit that we aimed to live a life
diametrically opposed to theirs.

It was interesting that we weren't able to tell them anything
about our life as it really happened. When you looked at it,
there was hardly anything to say. Our life barely existed, as
if it had been left behind in some secret argot, where I had
also left my real being, while this impostor sat at the table,
enumerated bland facts, nattered about traffic, and introduced
himself to her parents as me. His gaze wandered around the

flat. At Sanja's parents' there was nowhere to look—there was no empty space. Her mother had a morbid fear of open spaces and the flat was so crammed that there was hardly any air to breathe.

On our second morning there, Sanja suggested to her mother that they knock down the wall between the kitchen and the living room to gain more space, and I made the mistake of seconding the idea. Her mother glanced at me in consternation. She was used to her daughter having strange ideas but was disappointed that Sanja had found the same sort of guy. She immediately ridiculed the idea with her Mediterranean temperament. She spoke exclusively to Sanja— you could tell that she couldn't discuss such intimate topics as knocking down the wall with me. Probably Sanja wanted to appear a mature adult in front of me, so she kept contradicting her mother, and not just about the wall. You couldn't really call it an argument, more a mutual show of disrespect, which seemed to keep them cheerful in a way and create a special closeness. Their taunting and teasing actually showed how much they were at home.

I couldn't talk with her mother like that—I respected her—so I was condemned to silence. Also, my future mother-in-law kept her jabs and wise-talk exclusively for Sanja, not me, because she respected me.

Having fallen silent about the wall, I found it hard to talk at all. Our people are like that: they'd always prefer to build a wall than knock one down. They always liked having two rooms rather than one.

I spoke very cautiously with Sanja's dad, of course. He had disappointment written on his brow. Politics was his particular chagrin; all the parties were a letdown. He watched the news avidly, read the newspaper, and was disappointed time and time again. That seemed to be his main occupation. He wanted to know if we journalists were disappointed too. "Oh yes!" I exclaimed and mentioned a few practical examples. I felt a kind of need to join him in disappointment, but maybe he thought I even wanted to outdo him in that because I was a journalist in Zagreb and had the opportunity to get disappointed firsthand, so in a way he didn't want to listen. Whenever I opened my mouth he'd start explaining how much Zagreb was out of step with the situation on the ground, which was one of the things that disappointed him most.

I sipped beer, slowly, and watched the news. The mass of empty beer cans grew, rattling in the rubbish bin until they were crushed down into a smaller pile.

I thought of telling Sanja that one actually didn't look so lost among all the little tables at my parents' place, after a drink or two.

"My folks have got a nice courtyard and a garden, you'll see," I said cheerfully.

Then we arrived and I saw the garage. They'd told me about the new garage and were pleased with themselves for fitting it perfectly into the courtyard. Using a remote control, they proudly opened up the garage as if they were officially opening a new production line.

Yep, my folks had become bourgeois, so to speak, and we sat there like we had at Sanja's folks'. The new edifice that had replaced the courtyard stuck out like a sore thumb. And you couldn't say anything against it. I was about to say a word and they came down on me like a ton of bricks. How dare I cruise in from Zagreb and lecture them—from Zagreb, mind you. Zagreb with its holier-than-thouness was like a red rag to a bull. They needed that new addition: our garage is our castle.

My mom whispered to Sanja, forging a female alliance, that she didn't need to listen to me all the time because men were stupid: let them have their whims. My father generally

followed her remarks with a smile, and here and there
heckled his old lady just for fun, which Sanja was supposed
to find amusing. I tried to mediate these conversations as far
as possible by drawing attention to myself, but my parents
only had eyes for their daughter-in-law because, seeing as I'd
brought her, it was clear to them that we were going to get
married.

Then we were back in our rented flat. Things had stopped
evolving and I didn't know exactly what we'd think up next,
what lifestyle. We just had to avoid repeating the same old
patterns, I told Sanja. We had to break through in a new
direction, bore a tunnel, build a bold viaduct, whatever.

But then Boris had popped up, a feature in the landscape
like my parents' garage. I simply couldn't explain to her the
whole depth of the problem, so I turned the laptop toward her.
"Read some of his stuff and tell me what you think."

From: Boris <boris@peg.hr>
To: Toni <toni@peg.hr>

Resistance is removed like a wart with a laser. I guess all
this looks like a film when you see it on TV, the desert is
just the right backdrop, as if you were colonizing Mars,
you have no idea if there's any life there, you search for
it, move on, there has to be something, at least bacteria
or remains, fossils, fossil fuels, who knows what,
you never know if the aliens have weapons of mass
destruction, what level of technology they're at.
Here's an embedded journalist, a Bush, Tudjman,
or Miloševic man, someone's fan, please circle the
correct answer, and he asked me what I thought about
weapons of mass destruction, if there were any, and
would they be used in the Battle for Baghdad. He

provoked me because everyone somehow realizes
that I'm an amateur, no idea how those pros tick, but
of course Saddam's boys don't have weapons of mass
destruction because you definitely wouldn't attack
them if they did, so never fear, we can be calm, I said
optimistically, and we toasted with alcohol-free beer.
The people love me. What more can I say? I feel
accepted, but then the storm begins, a wind from the
south brings eddies of dust and fine, fine sand, it fills
your mouth, nose and eyes, so we fled to the cars and
sat in those closed cars all day, sweating, you can't
see a thing, you don't dare to open a window, not
in your wildest dreams, not in your wildest fucking
dreams. The sand will make its way in, into your brain.
Inside it's unbearably hot, brain waves, frequencies,
bro, I wanted to call you just now to see what the
weather's like there, but they told us to be careful
with the Thuraya numbers because they could be
located, rocketed, and there's no point in me getting
charcoaled here just because of the weather.

Sanja smiled as she read. "He's just having fun."

"I don't know if he's gone crazy or not."

"I think it's tongue-in-cheek," she said.

"He's messing me around, the dickhead! If anyone's the
object of that humor, it's me."

"I don't find it all that weird, you know. He has no training
in your language. I think if someone sent me to tag along
behind the Yanks as if I was reporting on a sports event, I think
I'd kind of want to muck up too."

"OK, I know you're against the war."

"And why shouldn't I be? At least this guy is saying
something; your paper doesn't have any position on the war."

"So basically you mean he's being subversive?"

"Consciously or not."

So they were the subversive ones, and I represented the system; they were on the side of freedom, and me—of repression. Sanja laughed as she read more. So he's witty, and I have no sense of humor? And I have to rack away at the crud he's written to patch it up while the young 'uns could let it all hang out.

"I'd publish it like that," she said.

"I can't publish that. We're a normal newspaper, not a fanzine for nutters."

"Yes, you lay down what's considered 'normal,'" she said.

"Tell that to Ingo. Sounds like you're a bigger punk at home than on the stage."

"That was below the belt."

"You're lecturing me as if I'd just started thinking about all this today! I know all that stuff! But that's how I get paid, and I'm having to take out that fucking loan. I know what's possible and what's not!"

"I'm lecturing you? You keep talking. *Stop yelling.*"

The *Buena Vista Social Club* soundtrack sounded through the speakers. I'd seen the film and realized something was wrong with the Cubans. They were so much better than us.

I had a nose for talents and starlets, relatively gifted individuals with their hearts set on recognition and fame. Maybe the point was that for years I'd spent too much time in bars and knew every idiot. In a nutshell, I volunteered as the newspaper's human resources agent because whenever they needed someone young and enthusiastic they'd ask me.

That's how fresh blood arrived in journalism, including even the Chief. It may sound strange, but I picked him up too, straight from a bar, back in the dawn of the democratic changes, and led him by the hand to the paper. Poetically put, his success was faster than the wind. Because our country has great social mobility. We don't have a stable elite. Socialism destroyed the old elites—what little bourgeoisie and provincial aristocracy we had, war and nationalism in the '90s destroyed the socialist elite. And then democracy happened and the remnants of the nationalist elite had to be done away with.

Defeated elites can survive in nooks and crannies. Oh yes, they can conduct their businesses and pull the strings from the shadows; but out in the light of day, in representative media we constantly needed new people. New columnists and opinion-makers, new faces, new photos. So, in the ten years of feverish change we'd gone through three media paradigms: socialist, wartime, democratic.

Uncompromised people were in short supply. If until recently you'd listened to Lou Reed, worked as a waiter, or studied viticulture, you now had the opportunity to put forth those new values. Democracy, pop culture, slow food. Without questioning capitalism, of course—we're not Reds!—so there was nothing you could do about the privatization that was pushed through in the '90s by the shock troops of happiness. The dough was safely stashed away and young media cadres came along to portray an idyll of Europeanization and normalization. After all, what else is there to do after the revolution has been carried out and the dough tucked away? What we needed now was harmony, security, consumers, and free individuals who paid off their loans. We could promote a little hedonism too, let people enjoy themselves, but within limits, of course, so as not to displease the Church.

We were a new society, a society with constantly changing backdrops and new illusions. We were all new at the game. There was no House of Lords, landed gentry, or old bourgeoisie, only the former socialist working people

who'd spruced themselves up and now crowded forward in
a carnivalesque exertion, grasping for the stars. The Eastern
European post-communist version of the American dream did
exist. Success depended on chance amidst the general turmoil
and rapid repositioning. One of the ordinaries would be shot
into orbit. But who?

The Chief had outdone me, there was no doubt about that.
He became the great editor, while I was still collecting losers
by the roadside. And Pero, as we know, was no longer the same
person.

I'll never forget when Pero began to progress; for a time he
shunned my gaze, greeted me hurriedly, avoided sitting at the
same table as me. Had he forgotten who'd brought him to the
office in the first place?

I always made the same mistake: I inadvertently reminded
people of what they used to be.

Later I accepted him as a new person who had nothing to
do with the waiter from Limited. Then he, in turn, accepted
me again.

Logically thinking, I must have changed in some way too,
despite my best efforts. If Pero became my boss nothing could
stay the same.

I mentioned these things to Sanja, I think, but always with
a laugh and a joke, as if I was wafting in a higher universe safe
from so-called social values. Stuff from the world of careers
didn't interest her anyway. She only saw love. Our love and love
in the wider world. Ecology. Genuineness. She loved me just
the way I was. It was only recently that she'd begun to follow
the Career column of the horoscope.

And now, through nervous conversations, we'd begun
to arrive at it, at the context—like in *Alien*, when the crew,
after initial arrogance, begins to grasp the magnitude of the
problems lurking in the cave in that distant galaxy.

Now, after Boris, it was crystal clear that my voluntary mediation in human resources was extremely stupid. Sanja compared it to her experience of volunteering in the alternative drama group Zero. Her circles from the Academy had gathered there, full of enthusiasm, only to break up in rancor in the winter, with everyone feeling they'd been used by a bunch of thankless idiots.

The fact that there was no cash caused feelings to get all muddled. Who knows why, but doing away with monetary accounts inevitably leads us onto the path of emotional reckoning. Wherever there's no dough you open an emotional account: you seek some form of acknowledgment. But how are you going to measure that? In the end everyone feels the others owe them something. That was the end of Zero. Everyone quarreled with everyone else, the expletives were as foul as foul could be, and Sanja felt used; she decided that in the future she'd only act when she was paid.

To tell the truth, it bugged her a bit that she'd departed from her youthful ideals so quickly.

I felt like that myself when I dropped out of Drama. I was working for various newspapers and, parallel to that, listening to the bullshit of pocket-monied students at uni. The longer I worked, the more avant-gardist they became. We read the deconstructionists and tried to apply them to the field of drama. We had conversations verging on the schizophrenic.

I was angry at my parents for canceling my pocket money and making fun of my efforts at deconstruction. I was angry at the Zagreb alternative bimbos who sooner or later would become part of the local glamour scene. I was angry at the proles and the elite, at work and art—having ended up somewhere in between. I was someone who hadn't managed to penetrate the haze between all those cultural classes, all those people who were so damn convinced of their own authenticity. I was angry at myself because I couldn't express myself.

When Sanja left volunteering on the fringe I told her it was the right thing to do. She agreed. There was no other option, and if there was, it had to stay a secret, like masturbation in the bathroom at work, or me voluntarily sticking my nose into human resources.

Here I channeled my anarchic instincts and enriched the staff profile with unexpected guests like Boris, whom no tie-wearing staffer would ever have chosen. That was a holdover of my subversive tendencies from the days when I used to sing along with Johnny Štulić—fellow rebel and Yugoslavia's answer to Joe Strummer:

> *The street is lined on either side*
> *With office buildings tall*
> *Bureaucrats creep and teem*
> *Help, oh help*
> *It makes my flesh crawl.*

Like bacteria that become resistant to antibiotics, my rebellion mutated during the search for enjoyment under capitalism. Find yourself a little hole in the system, have your fantasies, and live on them, cultivate them like people grow a little bit of pot in a secret place.

The whole business with Boris was prime evidence that my idea of subversion was only doing harm to myself. But I didn't want to talk about it with Sanja in these terms. I didn't see any way of saying all that to her without it having major consequences. I thought it'd have a disastrous effect on her image of me—and of us. She believed we were special.

Being very young and an actress, Sanja could still enjoy everything. Her identity was dynamic. But I couldn't change as the wind changed. I felt everything was in the process of being defined and I was developing my own vision of the future, a vision that haunted me. At first glance it was nothing terrible, everything seemed down to earth. But I saw a putrid life in a putrid atmosphere with people who were half putrid. We met at work-related parties and children's birthdays, sipping beer and slagging off about this and that, about our government and the Americans, and then the fun began as we talked about minor victories we encountered at work. I saw people buying new washing machines, fitted kitchens, and hi-fis to listen to rock, buying shelves and arranging their CDs on them. I saw them exchanging exotic recipes, showing photos from summer holidays, and talking about Istrian stone houses. I saw people to whom I was afraid to show pity, I saw happiness becoming compulsory and everyone saying fantastic, fantastic, fantastic. I saw them park, park, park in front of fenced-in holiday cottages where they were holding their child's birthday party, and someone would say, Where have you been? I haven't seen you for ages! I saw myself among them making a few sick jokes, but taking care not to insult anyone, especially not all of us together.

At 7:29pm a huge clock appeared on the screen. It happened every day. I don't know if the evening current-affairs program begins like that everywhere or only in former socialist countries.

The TV showed the entrance of Rijeka Bank and zoomed in at the bank's logo above the entrance.

There was a problem with the bank—that much was clear if they were filming it like that. Money had inexplicably disappeared.

Tomorrow they'd reproach me for us not reporting it first. Why hadn't our sources alerted us?

I rubbed my eyes. Sanja made a movement beside me, but when I looked I saw she was sleeping.

Now for Baghdad. The reporter looked me in the eye and told me the situation there was returning to normal.

I switched to Bosnian TV. Easier to watch the Bosnians. Their mess was essentially the same, only much worse, so their view of things calmed me a little. They announced a feature on the recipient of Police Officer of the Year.

My mobile rang.

"Who is it?" Sanja asked, raising her head.

"One of the many."

She just sighed with irony.

"Markatović," I said. "I'll call him later."

"I bet he was born with a mobile in his hand."

"That's just his business side."

"Is there anything else to him?"

✉

From: Boris <boris@peg.hr>
To: Toni <toni@peg.hr>

The rate of advance is now 30-40 kilometers a day, resistance is eliminated from the air, and I'm still eating the biscuits I've lugged with me from Kuwait. They stick in my throat, I bum water wherever I can, otherwise I'm always drinking warm Coca-Cola, there's enough to throw away here, as if Coke is sponsoring this whole rally. I'm on a Coca-Cola high, soon all the bubbles will come out on my skin as blisters!

Sanja took the remote, flipped through the channels, and stopped at a police series.

I touched her neck like I was gently massaging her. I got behind her and kissed her on her uncovered lower back, and she gave a wiggle of pleasure. She turned around, kissed me on the mouth and stroked my hair. She leaned against me and looked at me pleadingly as if she wanted to take a rest from everything.

On the screen a forensic expert, who also happened to be a psychiatrist, prepared a psychological profile showing that the man they were seeking was a sex maniac. She argued that he actually wanted to be caught and was therefore leaving traces, and he was terribly intelligent, which opened up a whole gamut of potential plots for scriptwriters. Series like this one were becoming ever more popular. A whole civilization lived in fear of sex maniacs because civilization is a sex maniac.

I stroked her back and then moved down lower.

"Hmm. You know, I have to get ready. The dress rehearsal's at eleven," she said.

The phone rang, the landline this time.

Sanja answered, then held out the phone. "It's some woman."

I took the receiver. "Hello."

"H'llo, guess who this is?"

I shat myself. "Milka?"

I could see that strong, stocky woman, vintage hairstyle from the age of the first moonwalk.

"Thought you'd recognize me!"

"H-how could I not?"

Milka was my mother's eldest sister, but I hadn't seen her since she fell out with my ma in a dispute over an extended-family inheritance; neither of them stood to inherit anything, they just sided with different camps, which ultimately led to them testifying against each other in court.

Milka was also Boris's mother.

"So how are you?" I thought it better to use the formal "you" to help maintain distance.

"Alive and kicking. And you?"

"Good."

"Do you know why I'm calling?"

"To do with Boris I suppose?"

"Where is 'e? What's goin' on?"

"He's in Iraq."

"I know that much. But he don't call me, like. What a shameful boy. I dunno what to do with 'im. Does he call you?"

"He was in touch just a few days ago."

"And where is 'e now?"

"In Baghdad."

"I shouldna let 'im go there," she whimpered and started sobbing.

"Listen . . ."

"Poor wee lad. You shouldna sent 'im there."

"No, Aunt Milka, listen! He asked me. I didn't ask him to go, let alone tell him to go."

"E's mad!" Milka exclaimed. "Believe me, the lad ain't in 'is right mind."

Then she fell silent. I very much wanted to console her, so I started defending that black sheep.

"Maybe he simply can't call you. Do you have email?"

"What?"

"Email."

"No, where would I get that from? But, 'e could've phoned me. Ain't 'e got a mobile?"

"It doesn't work there," my voice trembled as I lied. "It's pretty chaotic."

"So you think everythin's OK?"

"Everything's under control."

She sighed again. "All right then. Sorry to trouble you. Muvvers will be muvvers—we worry."

"I know, Aunt Milka, it can't be helped. Talk to you soon."

Talk to you soon? Why the hell did I say that?

"There are cool people and hot people," I said to Sanja." Cool people let you live your own life, but hot people don't. With them, everything always turns out communal. Open a little door for them and they'll burst through by the million."

"Don't think about that now," Sanja said as she got ready to go out. "He might get in touch tomorrow."

"There are more of them for sure. We're cool people who live in a hot country, that's our problem."

"That's so true," she said, looking at herself in the mirror.

"The idiot hasn't called her even once—their relationship must be a bit of a dog's breakfast. She acts as if I had personally mobilized him. Fucking hell, as if I'm George bloody Bush."

"Hey, don't get so upset. Nothing's happened yet, has it?"

"No, it hasn't. Unless they drag me into their shit. Now I have to become part of their madness."

"You don't have to."

"Like hell I don't. You don't know Milka."

"Calm down."

"Everyone can just go and stick it. Is this what they call life? This is shit!"

"No, that's not true."

"Oh really?" I sneered. "Why don't we go and see that flat? Can you explain that to me?"

"What's that got to do with it?"

"Everything. It's got everything to do with it."

"What do you think, that I'm avoiding—"

"I don't think anything!' I thundered.

She looked away.

"Sorry," I said.

"All this drives me round the bend, sorry."

"Don't take out your anger on me anymore."

"I won't. It was out of line."

I went to her, kissed her on the shoulder.

"It's OK," she said. "I have to get going."

"Good luck tonight." I held her arm. "You can do it. You'll be great."

She hugged me. Tight, like I was a traveler returned from a distant journey. Happy that I was back.

From: Boris <boris@peg.hr>
To: Toni <toni@peg.hr>

Terrific, terrific, terrific! The Tomahawk missile introduced during the First Gulf War is still a terrific miracle of technology that flies, flies, flies just below the speed of sound, follows the terrain and hits a programmed target with a 450kg warhead up to 1,600km away. How beautiful it is to write that? Nothing hurts! The US Navy has around 1,000 Tomahawks and each one of them costs $600,000, so I can tell you, it's simple: you've gotta have a good fucking reason to want to hit someone with it, I mean, to fire at someone with a thingo worth $600,000, you have to have a damn good financial reason, otherwise it's not worth it, cuz. It's no good if a missile's worth more than what it hits. I've realized that's the main problem with American involvement around the world. You can't target every idiot. You can only fight wars where it's worth it. In Africa, for example, it really doesn't make financial sense. Whatever you hit is cheap. The damage in no way justifies the cost

of the missile. That's the problem with wars in the
Third World—low real-estate prices. They'd say you're
producing losses.

That's right, losses. Look how far it's gone. The
Africans ought to develop a bit, they have to be given
a boost, then they can be targeted. But it's pointless
the way things are at the moment. There's no sense to
it, and sense is the most important thing.

When the price of Tomahawks comes down the world
will change. When they come up with advanced
weaponry at an acceptable price, the world will be
different. Then the Yanks will also be able to intervene
where there's no money. But the question is when
that's going to happen. I think advanced weaponry
will stay expensive. Purely so that not everyone blasts
away at everyone else. If some down-and-out guy
got hold of a Tomahawk, everything would be up shit
creek. At least the rich go round their properties and
do a cost-benefit analysis first. But if a poor man has
weapons—I mean weapons and nothing else—uh-oh!
It really makes you want to fire on them yourself to
show you have a weapon as well. You simply can't
resist, you have to fire a bit. That's the problem with
the wars of the poor. You decide what you're going to
do with this, but I have to philosophize a bit; I've got
nothing else to do here.

The Serbs, for example, the losers, were warring for
all of the '90s, but they don't have a fiscal plan. They
fight and fight and get more and more fucked up. That
can't happen to the advanced nations. Our Serbian
bros blam away their resources, run up huge losses,
and then they don't know what to do. They seize half
of Bosnia and then sit there doing nothing.

You know, all that stuff ruins people mentally as well.
After the war and all that wretched stress a man
wants to have a bit of a rest. And not, fucking hell,
drudge away to make up for the damage. Who'll force
a warrior to work? That's an old Indian question. You

can't stick him in a reservation to sow corn. Geronimo
and his braves would rot there—as soon as it was time
for a scrap they'd have to go to the shrink. As long
as the shit is going on, as long as you're taking rock
after rock, hill after hill, ditch after ditch, thicket after
thicket, as long as you're pushing back the borders, it
all looks like you're going somewhere, like things are
evolving, like there's some perspective.
That's a serious problem for us pauper warriors! We
have no idea what to do when the war is over. Be a
philosopher? A priest? Who? What?

"You called?" I said to Markatović in place of a greeting.

"Have you got time for coffee? It's important."

Why couldn't he invite me out for a beer like normal people
do? Why were we constantly meeting like two over-important
businessmen?

"Are you going to drag me into another scheme?" I asked.

"Now Dijana's calling, I have to get that. I'll call you back in
a minute."

When the phone rang again it was the landline. It couldn't
be Markatović, he always called me on my mobile. I stood
above the phone and looked at it. Finally it fell silent—and
then started again. It was still ringing as I left the flat, slamming
the door as if I'd just had a falling-out with someone.

By the time Markatović called I was already in the car.

"Meet me at Limited," I told him.

"That's not exactly on my route."

"Too bad, I've just found somewhere to park."

"Man, I'm in a suit, with a tie too," he complained.

"Well, take it off then. If it's that important, I'm here."

I worked my way through the crowd, checking to see if I
knew anyone. Old lounge lizards used to hang out here, but

our generation of fighters and survivors was becoming fewer
and fewer. We'd suffered heavy casualties, no doubt about it.
In spite of the crowd, if someone from the old guard had rung
up and asked me who was there, I'd have said, "There's no one
here."

There was nothing else to do but watch the girls, wait for
Markatović, and wonder what he'd come up with now. It
seemed he feverishly thought up jobs just to keep people at the
table and delay going home. He loved Dijana, he said, but he
just couldn't bring himself to go home.

Still, I was glad when the old goth came in.

"Anyone here?" He winked to me after glancing around.

He ordered a double whiskey with lots of ice. When his
drink came he suggested moving to a table in the back, so we
could talk.

"How's work then?" he asked.

"I'm waiting to see what happens. And you? How's your
poetry coming along?"

"Slowly. I work on it when I have time." He glanced around
furtively. "Did you see what happened today on the stock
market?"

"Don't mention the stock market. Is that too much to ask?
Same with Dolina. I don't want to hear about him."

I was on the verge of telling him that it'd be best for him to
go home. I was sick of watching him turn into a workaholic,
while running away from his wife and constantly talking
about other things. More, it annoyed me that we had to
seclude ourselves at a corner table. I didn't like the static view;
I wanted things to be moving in front of me. That was the
Mediterranean in me. Everywhere in the Mediterranean, from
North Africa to Venice to Istanbul, people are used to watching
the waves coming in, they're accustomed to that rhythm. In
the Mediterranean you can sit anywhere—on stairs, a stone

wall, or the ground, and aimlessly watch the pulsing of the sea. Markatović was a continental guy and had no feel for that.

"What's up with you?" he said.

"Either go home or let's drink like men."

"Have I done something to offend you?" he asked.

"I'm a bit tense."

Markatović knocked back his whiskey and waved for another round.

"Everything's fucked," he griped.

"Tell me about it."

"You, too? What's up?"

"I recommended a blockhead to be our correspondent in Iraq. He's gone there, and now I can't reach him, he's not answering."

"So what are you going to do now?"

"I'll wait. It's not too late, he could still get in touch. Luckily, we are a weekly newspaper, not that he knows it."

"You shouldn't get worked up in advance. Look, one day a guy came back, some kind of cameraman, and get this, he'd smuggled golden pipes out of Saddam's house in Tikrit. I heard that from an antique dealer."

His mobile rang again. It was Dijana.

If I'd had to describe his voice, I'd have said he was trying to sound soporific. It sounded like a ballad about the wide, blue sea.

"Really, I'm with Toni. In Limited. We're just finishing something." A blast of music: *You gotta fight for your right to paaarty*.

He put down the phone and blew out a tired plume of smoke.

"She's been so nervous recently," he said.

"You work too much."

"I have to," he sighed and became pensive. "Have you heard the news about Rijeka Bank?"

"Yes, dammit."

"It's serious," he muttered.

I rolled my eyes. "How wonderful it is when people use media events to flee from themselves! All those affairs sound so important and no one can stop you from talking about them, even if you're fucked up for a completely different reason."

"Someone knew before the others and sold up. Someone from the bank for sure."

"And now what? Do you want me to write a book about it?"

"The shares will plummet," he predicted.

"Yes," I said, grinning, clinking my glass against his. "Probably to zero."

"Think so?" He sighed like the loneliest man in the world. "I'm in it in a big way."

"Do you have shares in Rijeka Bank, RIJB-R-A?"

"Heaps."

"When did you put your money in?"

"This morning," he said, staring at his glass as if he was going to smash it against his head.

"Shit, you were still on that coke from last night. Did you sleep at all?"

"I went into it quite rationally. It's a bank that was bought by the Germans, fucking hell."

There you go: even the Germans were no longer what they used to be. As soon as they came here they got corrupted.

"I stuck in a heap of cash, even the lump I got from Dolina this morning. I've been following the shares. My computer has a live feed and I saw it all happen. The trading was strong. I thought of catching the wave and exiting again as soon as the share went up a little; I withdrew some dough like that two months ago, but a smaller amount. I wanted to take advantage of having cash in my account."

"Hang on, you mean the share went up this morning?"

"Yes, but then I twigged what was happening. The bank's management had artificially created demand so they could get rid of their investment. Obviously the bank itself bought their shares, and we others joined them. The shitheads knew about the losses. It was a diversion, like Tito's at the Battle of the Neretva."

"Talk about getting screwed!"

"Now, I can try and sell in the morning. But that will be such a loss."

There goes my guarantor, I thought.

"The other solution would be to wait for them to come in and overhaul things," he continued. "Bayerische Landesbank is prominent."

"In Germany, yes," I said soberly. "But I think you'll find it's a different ball game here. They could just get up and go."

"Then the Croatian government has to intervene— someone has to."

"But it's no longer government-owned."

"True, but heaps of firms in the Rijeka region are attached to the bank, so I reckon the government can't afford to let all of them go down the plughole together with me."

"Sounds logical enough," I said sympathetically.

"Should I wait or not?" he asked.

I saw how much he trusted me. It was awful.

"I don't know," I said.

"What does your instinct tell you?"

"I don't know. It's hard when you lose so much. I don't know—I'd probably wait. But that's just a gut feeling."

"You'd wait?" The shine returned to his eyes.

He rummaged in his pockets.

"Have you tried that coke?" he asked.

"I'm saving it for tomorrow."

"I'm going to freshen up a bit," Markatović announced and headed for the bathroom.

From: Boris <boris@peg.hr>
To: Toni <toni@peg.hr>

There's nothing here to buy, smoked my last two cigarettes, no kiosk anywhere, only tanks, APCs, and the desert, no one sells ice cream, nor is there that Muvver Courage driving a cart. I'd like to call and hear more about your girlfriend the actress, but they told us to be careful with Thuraya numbers because we can be located, and I don't want to get frazzled just because of theater, though I respect it, I really do.

When Markatović came back from the toilet he said, "What were you saying? Your guy in Iraq isn't getting back to you?"

"The idiot also happens to be a cousin of mine," I said.

"I had fun like that with my dad. After his firm was bought up by a crook I tried to employ the old man so he wouldn't wallow around in depression. But he drove me completely nuts. He has no idea, meddles in everything, and is constantly calling me and giving me advice, like, fatherly stuff. And he's begun to drink in a big way. I'm not giving him anything more to do. But I can't just sack him."

"What are you going to do with him?"

"Wait until he retires. He's got two more years."

DAY THREE

There were Eskimos all around me, doing me a great service by burying me in ice so one day someone would be able to dig out my preserved body when my ailment had a remedy. Once their job was complete, the Eskimos left, singing, and that Coca-Cola drinking polar bear lumbered up. He was followed by a whole family of polar bears, who sat on my frozen tomb.

"Hmm, maybe I'm not quite dead after all," I thought.

Their furry bums were hot and the ice melted beneath them. I lay there waiting for them. At that point the alarm went off.

While brushing my teeth I checked my email. I was still half-asleep. I'd won £206,000 in the British National Lottery. There was email from Kofi Edwards, manager of Fidelity Bank in Nigeria, where $20,000,000 US had got stuck in an account, and old Kofi was asking me to do him a favor and

withdraw the money for him. Good news all round. But
nothing from Boris.

Sanja came in. She always used to laugh at the toothpaste
foam dribbling down my chin, but I could see she didn't want
to laugh. She was carrying a newspaper and I twigged straight
away that she was in it.

She'd probably been practicing that nothing doing
expression on the walk back from the kiosk.

"Wow, that wouldn't be our first interview, would it?"

She laughed at her own awkwardness. This opening up of
vanity—that's intimacy for you, I thought.

Beneath the headline OUR CHEMISTRY HAPPENED ON STAGE
sat a photo of Sanja and Jerman at rehearsal. His arm was around
her waist. OK, calm down, I said to myself, it's only his arm
around her waist. But the GEP guys had really done it with that
title; my heart hummed like a diesel on a winter morning.

"It seems the chemistry also worked between you and Jerman."

"Don't be crazy."

Bloody gutter press—the male chauvinism of the media
had never repelled me as much as now. There were two more
photos: stilted studies showing her alone. Over the past four
years she'd developed some fine feminine curves. The caption
said she had the stuff to be a star. They were obviously thinking
of a sex symbol and a vamp.

In her everyday appearance Sanja rebelled against such
an image of herself. She was a proponent of unisex youth
fashion: jeans and sneakers. But now that defensive stance was
crumbling before my eyes.

She was wearing her costume from the play—cheap and
raunchy. That was her role, that's the way it was. But that feline
look, that bare waist, that perky breast peeking out through the
scanty blouse, that thigh. And there you go: I felt the stirrings
of an erection. I grabbed her bum, kissed her neck.

She pushed me aside. "The photos are all that count, is that it? All the reactions are going to be like that, I know it."

In the interview they did begrudgingly mention Brecht in the introduction, and asked about the play in the very first question, just to be polite. And then: "How do you get on with Leo Jerman, your main acting partner?" She said they got on great. "You have one nude scene and quite a few skin-on-skin situations in the play. Is it hard for you to act them?" That was her job, she said, and she approached it professionally. "Do you practice those love scenes, and if so how?"

Here the interview descended into soft erotica and didn't return to drama. Somehow they arrived at her "current relationship." She said she wanted to preserve her privacy, and I fully supported her in that. But I was just a tiny bit disappointed that she didn't mention me. Then they asked if she'd appear completely nude if she had the offer and if the film so required. "For a good film, a good role, and good money— yes." Then they asked her how important sex was in her life and if rehearsals affected her sex life. "Ha, ha, ha, a bit."

It was all like that: nothing about anti-globalism, nothing about George Bush, nothing about what we philosophize about at home. My little Sanja didn't even notice that she'd been sucked into the interview-with-a-blonde genre. She walked into it like Eastern Europeans into capitalism. Why, only yesterday she'd been lecturing me about the media, how they're the hand that shapes you. If you're a young actress who has to show her tits in a renowned theater on the periphery of Europe—not even Brecht will get you out of the shit!

Let's be realistic, I didn't know how she could have been careful except by giving no interviews at all. Actresses are at the mercy of gossip-mongering journalists—if she'd waited to be interviewed by a theater critic she could end up waiting until she was a pensioner. Critics have never interviewed actresses because they don't know a thing about acting. No one knows a thing about acting, although it is ubiquitous.

Maybe that's exactly the reason, I thought. Acting is a paradigm of our age: it's the quintessence of freedom of choice. No one is obliged to inherit an identity now, everyone can invent themselves and imitate Kurt Cobain, Madonna, or Bill Gates. There were times when you were born a serf and died a serf.

Just yesterday I'd been reading about Jimi Hendrix: how he tried to find himself and how he invented himself. Even in the summer of 1966 when he played at Café Wha? in New York, Hendrix wanted to look like Bob Dylan. He always had curlers in his suitcase and he straightened his hair to try and create a Dylanish hairdo.

No one in America thought a black could be a rock musician. Essentially there was no Hendrix at all until he arrived in London and was received as a marvel, an exotic species. So he chucked the curlers and tried to look as eccentric as possible; he adopted an afro and began to buy stupid clothes in secondhand shops like Granny Takes a Trip and I Was Lord Kitchener's Valet. He got a bit carried away with the attention and became Jimi Hendrix.

That was a revolution. When you come up with a new role, a new persona, you change the culture. If the pieces of your mosaic fit together right you can really take off like Hendrix.

But I wonder if his father recognized him after it all came together for Hendrix.

There's no heredity. A son doesn't want to be like his father, a daughter doesn't want to be like her mother but like Madonna. When a daughter realizes at a certain age that she's behaving like her mother and not like Madonna, the battle is lost. But one part of the personality refuses to accept defeat. A parallel identity is in our dreams.

Acting is a fundamental survival technique. It's always been that way. But now the choice of roles is bigger—democratic. The range on the identity market is broad. That's why socialism failed. It didn't offer people enough options, enough masks, enough subcultures, or enough films. There were too few roles, too few images, too few shoes and sneakers. The range was almost medieval. There were even too few nations. Too few states. Too few variations and petty, narcissistic differences. Too few media outlets.

We're all actors now. We wear our costumes and perform in the wide world. The actor is the idol of our time, a symbol of freedom—freedom of choice. But every idol has to pay for being an idol. So why was I surprised? Actresses were the rightful prey of gossip-mongering journalists, just like the infantry is free to plunder in war.

"What's up? What are you thinking about?" Sanja said as we both sat there looking at the page.

"It's really strange to read the interview and see the photos. But I'll get used to it."

"You think it's a disaster?"

Waiting for me to answer, she turned the pages, excited by that light and bouncy image of her.

"No, not a disaster. That's the nature of the light interview. That's what it is. Are you happy?"

"I don't know now. I thought you'd be glad."

"I just find it a bit strange, that's all."

"Same here."

"You'll get used to it."

"Two whole pages," she seemed surprised.

"Not bad for starters."

She read on, alternately beaming and frowning.

I told myself all that mattered was that I knew who she was. What did I care about how the public saw her, what they'd say about her down at the pub?

She sang a line from a popular song: "Life is mad but I'm no quitter / Make me coffee, black and bitter . . ."

> ✉
>
> From: Boris <boris@peg.hr>
> To: Toni <toni@peg.hr>
>
> Nothing for me to fuck here in bloody Iraq. There was a Lebanese girl, a reporter, who bestowed on me two or three female glances, the first in ages, but then she left abruptly with her team as if muvver had called her to lunch. Those Lebanese girls are my only hope, they're liberal by desert standards, but the mirage shattered as her jeep drove away, a leaden mirage in my dusty desert heart, and I, wretch that I am, just stood and watched.

On the way to work I passed by the Last Minute Travel Agency. Past Thailand, Kenya, Cuba and the rest, thinking I should buy a trip somewhere far away and disappear like Boris. But I'd just decided to settle down—to buy a flat and put down roots! That is what I want, isn't it?

Anymore, no one knew how to live.

We've been through communism, war, and dictatorship. Constant brain-ironing. Your circumstances adjust miraculously when you live in systems like that and you don't have the dough for big experiments. Your life shrink-wraps around you and you tread a narrow path; you hold course and wait for the storm to blow over.

I knew the ones in power were to blame for everything. That was my alibi. I wasn't responsible for their mess. I was trying to live my life while bogged down in that shit. So I sat in front of the TV and cursed every single one of them for having kept me on a short leash for so long. But now things had slackened dangerously.

Finally the time had come: normalization, they called it. Democracy. I could still pretend the ones in power were to blame for everything but the feeling was no longer convincing. The terror had abated. It was a shock to my system. The past had been easier, in a way. Now no one assumed responsibility. Where had the establishment terrorists gone? I felt strangely forlorn in my decisions.

Six months after Franjo Tudjman died I ended up at the psychiatrist's. He was the last one who raved at us, the last one who I was longing to be rid of. After that I took Xanax for a while. I was in transition like the country itself. Hey—I saw the light—now I was supposed to be a subject and be at the center of things. I had to act and choose.

But in my head the ghosts of those old terrorists taunted me: You're incompetent. You're gutless. You're no one. How are you going to live now? Let's see you choose! Marriage, children, apartment? Drugs, alcohol, macrobiotics? Christianity, meditation? Activism, anti-globalism, hedonism? Thailand, Malaga, pornography? Group sex, glamour? Shares, betting shops, building societies? Cuba, Kenya?

All the options gutted me. Every day on my way to work I drove by the Thailand advert, and I wanted to blow a fuse, keep going, bellowing a rock song to dispel the spirits that tied me to this place. My head was full of all those seas and oases, idyllic places where you could sit and sip cocktails in peace beneath a canopy, in a straw hat, without any trace of this existence, so you could pretend you were someone else.

At the office I sat down at a table covered in newspapers. Headlines: STUDENT MAKES IT TO A MILLION BUT GOOFS ON THE NAME OF FISH; THE MAGNIFICENT TEN WHO WILL LEAD CROATIA INTO THE EU; JOURNALISTS LEAVE IRAQ; ONE MORE BOAT FULL OF AFRICAN IMMIGRANTS SINKS; GENERATION P: HOW PEPSI WON OVER SOVIET CHILDREN.

I surfed the net, trying to relax by watching a webcam showing the peak of the Mexican volcano Popocatépetl. The hangover wasn't going away. I got up, walked past the lifts and ordered a Red Bull at the little café—a tiny booth squeezed in beside the staircase. A corpulent woman sat in the foyer, wearing the introspective expression that you see in doctors' waiting rooms. She reminded me of Milka, so I got out of there quickly.

Back in my office, I checked email again but still nothing from my cousin. Perhaps I wasn't patient enough. I thought about that woman waiting doggedly and realized that those are exactly the kind of people who were able to put up with socialism. They were a generation that stuck it out on waiting lists for housing and were then rewarded when the government gave them a flat. Waiting was a worthwhile business. It had become second nature to them. But today there's no more waiting for one's rights, there's a different sense of time. We're nervous. Speedy. We drink Red Bull so it will give us "wiiings." That's our generation.

I dialed Boris's Thuraya number. They connected me via London. A recorded voice in Arabic came on before it rang. Nothing.

I sent him another email: "Please get back to me. I know I offended you. Get back to me immediately, please, or I'll have to start a search for you. Stop horsing around now, things are getting serious. Please!"

Page 10 of GEP's newspaper: HERO OF THE PEACE. A young
Iraqi in a denim jacket with a white polo shirt and gel in his
hair, kissing Dubya's photo. On the same page, JOURNALISTS
LEAVE IRAQ, reported by our former colleague Rabar, who
wrote with irony, but finely honed, unlike my fool of a cousin:
"The war in Iraq, day 28." That's how it began, all nice and
clear. "The hotels are rapidly being vacated. Colleagues can
smell the next war coming and surmise 'What do you think,
are the Americans going to attack Syria or Iran? Or North
Korea?'" Rabar announced his moves, albeit imperceptibly for
the ordinary reader, but the insider could see the skill involved:
JOURNALISTS LEAVE IRAQ meant above all that he, Rabar, was
leaving Iraq. But our reporter was still there.

I phoned Sanja.
    "He still hasn't rung," I said.
    "Maybe you should talk about it with someone at the office."
    "I guess. I'll see."
    "OK then, bye, I have to go." She paused.
    Oh Jesus, her play. "Bye, good luck!"
    But she'd already hung up.
    She was right. I had to talk about it with someone here. But
where should I begin? By saying that he's my cousin? Or that
I'd falsified reports that ran in the paper?

With the inklings of a plan I headed to Secretary's office. He
was waiting for me.
    "I was just about to call you. We're off to see the Chief."
    "I need to talk to you about something."
    "It would've been great to find out about the Rijeka thing
earlier. Not exactly up to date, are we?"

I didn't have an explanation other than I'd forgotten about my actual job.

"It just caught everyone on the wrong foot," I said.

We stood there in the frame of his door. Or rather, I'd dug in there, and Secretary tried to get around me.

"We're off to see the Chief," he repeated.

"Listen, I have a few problems with the fellow in Iraq."

"Who?"

"You know who."

"Just forget about that now."

I had no choice; I set off after him.

He knocked on the Chief's door, poked his head in, and then entered.

We discussed Rijeka Bank. The Chief wanted a thriller about a bank robbery and Secretary was after a lively story with flesh-and-blood characters. I explained to them that their character had simply invested unwisely. He then tried to back out by taking a risk. He didn't report the disaster to anyone until the mess was perfect.

"The losses were then kept under wraps for a time, probably until the management sold its shares. That's their weak point now because it was fraud."

The Chief nodded.

"They had insider information and used it on the stock market. In America you go to jail for scamming like that, but here there's no law against it."

"What do you mean there isn't?" the Chief butted in.

"There's no law; parliament didn't pass it," I said.

"What? How's that possible?"

"I don't know," I admitted. "They went on and on about national pride—I can't remember."

"That's enough philosophizing," the Chief grumbled. "What's important is: Who stole the money?"

"The twit misinvested it. Scams are hard to prove."

"No no, it's not a scam," Secretary said.

Perhaps it wasn't the right time, but, thinking of Markatović, I started to talk about the responsibility of the media. Sensationalism in the economy was dangerous. We had to think about the ordinary shareholders, people who pray to God that everything ends well. This wasn't show business. If capital flees, if savers storm the banks, it's over. Our banks had collapsed that way before, I reminded them, and sometimes they'd even been destroyed intentionally.

Secretary rolled his eyes.

The Chief was in a no-nonsense mood. "First do this, then you can go into who destroyed the banks. And don't go on about responsibility, just be quicker in the future."

I tried objecting.

"It's agreed then," the Chief bulldozed. "All we need is a photo of the guy."

He cast a glance out the window.

"The sky's gone all dark," Secretary noted.

Pero nodded. "As if the shit will start to fall, as that famous Serb would have said."

They laughed.

"Kovačević," I said.

"What?" the Chief looked at me.

"The Serb. It was Kovačević, the playwright."

"Cut the crap, playwright! Where's the dough? Who's connected with the guy? Gimme that." He grabbed his coat and put it on.

"I've got another topic," I said, finally seizing the moment.

"What?"

"The Red Bull Generation. It's a phenomenological story about our—"

"Not now," he said.

"That's for a column. We have columnists for that," Secretary added.

"Yesterday the word was about creation," I said, stopping the Chief at the door. "We have to invent things. Politics is no longer in politics—where'd the hysteria go?"

He stopped.

"That's Red Bull: hype, fervor. We're anxious, like bulls being taunted by the red cape of the bullfighter. We run for nothing and it causes panic on the market, and all that—Red Bull covers that. Symbolically, I mean."

I'd never been pushy like that before. I'd always thought you're not allowed to be too pushy or you'll look like a real prole. You had to look relatively disinterested. Back in school we despised the overeager nerds and that attitude had stuck to me like a sidecar all through life. But I'd looked so disinterested for so long they weren't relying on me at all.

"Yeah, give it a try," the Chief said. "If you think you can do it. But not until next week. Now get on with the bank."

That woman was still waiting at the little café.

Curiosity got the best of me. "Are you waiting for someone?"

"'E was s'posed to play in Nantes but 'e didn' get to play."

"I'm sorry?"

"I'm Anka Brkić, muvver of the football star Niko Brkić," she let loose. "He was s'posed to play in Nantes."

"Isn't that mostly the case?"

"No no, 'e was s'posed to play," she caught her breath. "They invited him. But this manager, Marko Čatko, sold 'im to the Emirates, to Arabia. There was more money there. But 'e took all the money for 'imself—allegedly it's in the contract—and 'e also said Niko was 'is. My son was 'is!"

"Sounds nasty but if that's what the contract says."

I took a Vodka Red Bull and was about to go. But the woman had the kind of look—you just couldn't tear yourself away without feeling rude.

"Then my Niko, out of spite, din' wanna go to the Emirates: 'I'd rather stay 'ome and plough' 'e said. And now Marko Čatko and his people say they're gonna break his legs, so I've come to report it."

"Have you been to the police?"

"The police? Nah, Marko Čatko's brother, Ikan Čatko, is 'igh up in the police. I canna' do nothin'—I 'ave to go to the press."

I told her that she had to wait for Vladić, the guy who wrote about sports.

"Yes, they told me. I've been 'ere since this mornin'. There's not even nowhere to relieve myself."

"Vladić is sure to come by for a drink. "

So I showed the muvver of the football star Niko Brkić to the office bathroom and stood watch for her because I saw she was afraid. She thanked me profusely and went back to continue her wait.

I went back to my desk, the internet, and Popocatépetl. Out of the volcano's crater a wisp of smoke trailed up into the clear Mexican morning. The Centro Nacional de Prevención de Desastres constantly monitored seismic activity and the possibility of an eruption. The people around me phoned, wrote texts, rummaged through the rubbish, constructed reality, searched for events.

In that state of existential meditation I remembered the golden pipes from Saddam's house in Tikrit. Markatović said they'd been smuggled out by a cameraman working for foreigners. Perhaps Boris had got mixed up in business like that. Maybe he'd got hold of a Mesopotamian sculpture thousands of years old and was now hauling it through the desert. Locals are bound to try and flog all sorts of merchandise to foreigners. If a cameraman there is capable of smuggling Saddam's pipes, God only knows what Boris is going to bring back. Probably something worthless but big.

Then it hit me. Rabar would know about any Croatians still there. He wrote "Journalists leave Iraq" so he's bound to be on his way back or to have already arrived. He and I hadn't had a falling-out, so what did I care if he'd gone over to GEP?

I'd already pressed his number in my mobile's address list and got a connection before I realized the number was the one here in the office. The first digits were the same.

I hung up.

I needed his new number, the GEP mobile. I'd have to ring his wife and ask. But I didn't have his home number or his address. I didn't have anyone's address anymore. No one did.

I went to see the office secretary.

"Could I ask a you personal favor?" I said in a soft voice.

"Why are you sneaking up on me like this?" Jumpy woman.

"I need Rabar's number, or at least his address," I said.

"Rabar's?"

"Yes, it's something private. I loaned him a few things. Do you have his home number in the files?"

She gave me a conspiratorial look and then jotted down his number in silence, as if she were recommending me a dealer.

I winked and said, "Iraky peepl."

She didn't understand.

"That's, like, a password."

"And what do I have to say back?" she asked.

I caught Rabar at the airport in Frankfurt between two flights.

"Talk about out of the blue," he exclaimed. "How are things at home? Any rain?"

"Yes, I think there could be."

"I'd like that," Rabar declared. "Drizzle—or a downpour, a drencher, a deluge. Just give it to me. I want to feel the rain on my face, man. But here in Frankfurt there's nothing."

I told him we were working on a stupid piece, counting all the Croatians in Iraq so as to show that Croatia was playing an active role in world events. A long way of asking who of our people were still in Iraq.

After giving me some names, he said, "Listen, let me ask you. Have GEP and PEG reconciled since I've been gone?"

"No chance."

"A truce, even?"

"Nope. It's all still the same."

"Fucking hell. Well, bye." Rabar cut off, seemingly having remembered what the nature of our official relationship was. That's how it was during the war: while away you forget the local conflicts, but as soon as you're home the fights begin again.

I emailed the guys Rabar had mentioned, attaching a photo of Boris and asking them if they saw him to have him contact me immediately.

My mobile rang. The display said: RABAR.

"Hey, Rabar."

"Did you call earlier?"

Shit! It was Dario, apparently the novice had inherited Rabar's office number—the one I'd rung first.

"No. I must have pressed the wrong key."

"If you're after Rabar, he's gone over to GEP."

"No, really, it was just an accident."

"No hassle, mate, it's . . ."

"Cheers!" I cut him short.

Markatović called, whining straight away, "Any news about the bank? Do you think they'll save it?"

"I'm thinking about how to save my own ass here," I said.

"What do you think, should I wait?"

"How should I know? You haven't sold anything?"

"No. We agreed that I shouldn't."

I thought I'd scream at him and tell him we didn't have any bloody fucking agreement. Then I remembered that I'd screamed at him the night before, and toned it down. "Don't try and shift the responsibility to me. I have nothing to do with it. It's your money."

"I'll keep waiting," he said quietly.

"What choice do you have? And I'm waiting for that idiot to get in touch."

I clicked www.my-dosh.com, a stock market forum. Members bandied around information but what they wrote wasn't necessarily reliable. If one of them had RIJB-R-A shares he'd just find arguments to stop the avalanche. Someone under the pseudonym Cravat had reliable information that the government was going to financially rehabilitate the bank, otherwise it would be a political problem in the Rijeka region. Maybe that was Markatović. Another group showered him with abuse. The only support for him came from forum member Radex. Maybe that was Markatović too. The outgunned often use multiple pseudonyms to help create public opinion. Now I logged on with my handle, Trumbo Rich, and expressed moderate support for Cravat and Radex.

I started ringing the bigwigs. I'd interviewed the Minister of Economics twice while he was in opposition, so it would have been proper for him to answer my call. But he didn't. His spokeswoman took my breath away with her icy decorum and redirected me to the Office of the Vice President, where I chose a more aggressive tack and told them they'd better issue some kind of statement.

"What? Make something up?" she said. "We said everything at the press conference."

"You didn't say anything. Is the government going to back the bank or not?"

"The bank is not the government."

"There are rumors that they're handing it back to you. You didn't say anything about that."

"What we didn't say is pure speculation."

"But you didn't say 'no' either."

"We didn't say anything."

"Aha, just as I was telling you."

"I will not be provoked. I'll get back to you if the Vice President—"

"Good," I said.

I'd exhausted my journalistic aggression. I don't know how the others managed. I wasn't born for this muck.

I held my chin in my hands and stared out into the sky, which was still dark and overcast as it ruminated on the Red Bull generation with its horns and wings.

Then Charly dashed into the office. "Today is one big hassle." He had to give off signals of being overworked and terribly stressed so no one would think of giving him any. "I saw Sanja's interview, by the way. I'll go and see it."

Then he darted to his computer and started to type like a man possessed.

Finally Silva turned up too. She said she'd been talking to a woman waiting outside.

"The muvver of Niko Brkić who was s'posed to play in Nantes?" I asked.

Silva nodded, it seemed she was interested in writing it up, which surprised me. She wanted to take up some work that was a bit more serious. What did I think?

"What category would it go under?"

"Abuse in sport," she said.

She presented her theory: essentially, there was nothing positive in sport.

I nodded.

"In sport, like in modelling, they get you when you're a kid and have no idea what's going on. A mafia is milling around you the whole time. And he's still underage. You don't know how things work."

I knew they'd sent her to Milan when she was seventeen, she was there for a while but didn't make it into the top league. So she came back and pretended she'd made it abroad, because who'd know anyway? So she played the role of model, went out with shady types, figured in the "On the Heels of the Glitterati" column, earned a penny or two in local photo shoots, turned up at glamorous events, did cocaine, and was not all that far from elite prostitution. She was brought down to earth when she got pregnant by a source who wished to remain anonymous.

"Sports are absolutely feudal," Silva said resolutely.

I headed off to interview Mr. Olenić, who'd witnessed all the reforms of the last decades. I'd never have thought of him if he hadn't put in an advert for his inner-city flat. I'd gone to see the place a week and a half earlier; it was too expensive, but I made an appointment for an interview.

On my way, I picked up the photographer, Tosho, who volunteered to drive.

Out by the café, Anka Brkić was still holding her position. She was probably waiting for Silva now. I said hello as we went past.

When we got in the car, Tosho offered me a joint.

"I don't know, I'm hung over."

Still, I took two drags, and Tosho smoked the rest. We

weaved our way through the heavy traffic. Whenever someone blew their horn, Tosho would just take a deep breath and let out a weary "Aww man!"

The number of cars in Zagreb had increased enormously; credit lines were opened up after the war and the period of isolation, and after the decade of self-denial a period of compensation had begun. People bought things left, right, and center, shopping malls shot up like mushrooms after the rain and Croatia entered the WTO and similar organizations just when Naomi Klein published *No Logo* with the aim of spoiling our fun.

"Good grass. Who do you get it from?" I asked.

He hesitated.

"Never mind. Silly question," I said.

"No no, it's not a secret. I get it in the neighborhood from a kid who calls himself Joe. But, y'know, one day I saw 'im going into a bar and another mob was sittin' out the front. I called out, 'Joe,' and fuck—all of them turned to look!"

"No shit?" I said absently.

"When they're making a deal over their mobiles, everyone calls each other Joe because of the cops. That's how they speak to each other: Hi Joe, any news? Yeah, Joe, lots of shit goin' down."

"So they're all Joes."

"And now, y'know, if the cops were after Joe they could jus' forget it. There are fifty guys called Joe in the neighborhood. Now when I go into the bar, the waiter calls me Joe."

We finally fought our way through to the inner city; a fine rain had begun to fall, and by the time we got to Mr. Olenić's door we were a little wet and out of breath.

The old economist received us in his cold, dark flat; he was freshly shaved and wore a black suit with a white shirt and Bordeaux tie. He was over eighty but well-preserved, with the demeanor of a retired conductor.

We sat down at a coffee table in the living room. He spoke
about the economy under socialism. "Economic freedom
always resulted in internal political democratization. Starting
in the mid-fifties, we had introduced self-management in the
factories and workers councils and we tried to make a specific
kind of market. It wasn't like in the countries under Russians.
We were out of it, as you know. What was stopping the reforms
was the political bureaucracy class afraid of losing its power."

Mr. Olenić reminisced about times past with a slightly raised
chin, as if he was posing for one of the Old Masters. I poured
myself some of the whiskey he'd kindly put out on the table.
Quality stuff. He was so broke that he was selling his flat, but he
made a point of having whiskey. That's what I call attitude.

Tosho went around, crouching and standing up again. He
gave me a pained look in between two shots to signal that I
should animate Olenić a little. He wanted me to ask a question
that would aggravate the old man a bit—make him gesticulate
and show a lively face rather than speaking like a Russian
newsreader.

"You participated in the Yugoslav reform of 1965. Why did
it fail?" I asked.

"That reform was implemented by Kiro Gligorov, the
finance minister at the time." He raised a finger. "But you
can't say it failed. The international community assessed it as a
significant change in a Communist country. That was the end
of the command-planned economy." He held up his palms, as if
to ask: What more do you expect? "The people on the ground
started to make their own economic decisions. It brought
decentralization, but then there was the backlash."

"Yes, yes," I nodded, as Tosho snapped away.

"But, on the other hand, all that resulted in the constitution
of '74. The economy was behind that. Many in the old political
structure opposed the reforms, and the reckoning with

Aleksandar Ranković," he gestured as if sweeping a chessman from the board, "was an attempt to remove that resistance."

Tosho got up off his haunches; sweat beaded his forehead. "Brilliant."

"Pardon?" said Olenić.

"Ranković—the secret police, right?" Tosho said. "Good that you removed him."

"I didn't remove anyone." The old economist gave me a look as if at least I understood. "Those are processes."

"Yes, processes," I seconded.

Olenić stretched out his arms expressively. "You take out a piece here, and things collapse over there."

"OK, I've done my bit," Tosho said. "All the best, Mr. Olenić."

"See ya Joe," I quipped.

"Goodbye, Mr. Joe," the old economist said.

My throat was dry so I poured myself another whiskey. And a glass of water.

Olenić spoke about growth they had in the sixties and seventies, which stopped with the debt crisis in the eighties, and how with Tito dead there was no one with the authority to make decisions.

Finally he spoke about his involvement in Ante Marković's attempt to make an easy transformation to capitalism at the time the Berlin wall fell. "We announced privatization with workers as shareholders and we did a few of them. Today, some of them remain and are among the best companies in the country. We wanted privatization with a human face. The Slovenians achieved this, very different from the way things later turned out here. But Marković was blocked by Milošević. Once again, it was the political bureaucracy afraid of losing power, only now in nationalist garb. And so Yugoslavia collapsed and war started."

My mobile was ringing. Unknown number. I hoped it was a call from the ministry to do with Rijeka Bank.

"Just a minute, please," I said.

"It's me, Milka."

"Who?"

"Me. Aunt Milka. C'n you 'ear me?" she yelled.

"We'll have to talk later, I'm doing an interview now."

"Tell me where 'e is," she yelled. "Don't you tell me what to do—he's my only son!"

"I'm at an interview now."

I hung up. The phone rang again, blaring "Satisfaction." Olenić, that living witness of fall and ruin, sat there and looked at me.

"They're slow, but they're after me," I said.

"Sorry?"

"A quote from Admiral Mahić," I said.

"A naval commander?"

"Bosnian poet."

I turned off the phone.

I couldn't think of any more questions, so I poured myself another whiskey.

"Is that the end of your questions?" he asked, a smile breaking across his face.

"What do you think will become of Rijeka Bank?"

His smile evaporated. "You know that we are freed now. But, ironically, in this period of national freedom all our banks were sold to foreigners. So, we are freed of the capital too."

I was listening and thinking about getting free of Milka.

"It's like that in all small countries in Eastern Europe. Maybe that was the function of the freedom."

"An interesting way of putting it," I said.

"Let them think about that now!"

"But the Germans want to get rid of the bank now. The government could have it back."

"Listen," Olenić said, leaning in, "Yugoslavia was a sum total of small nationalities that united to fight the big ones. That's how we Croats got rid of the Italians on the coast and the Germans on the continent. We couldn't have done that by ourselves. Once we'd done that, we got rid of Yugoslavia too, i.e. the Serbs. Now we're going our own way, independently, but we're pitched against the big players again—the Italians and the Germans. That's the whole story."

"A story full of the suffering of innocents," I said, taking a sip of whiskey.

"The Italians and the Krauts have now taken over all our banks. Of course, when I say 'Krauts' I mean the Austrians as well. The Hungarians are also in the wings; they're not as significant, although there is the oil giant INA."

"Let's return to Rijeka Bank. The Germans are offering to give it back. Do you think the government will take it?"

Olenić went to the window. He opened the curtains and looked out. Rain pelted the glass.

"All that's irrelevant, at a deeper level. I helped build up socialism. That was essentially an act of resistance to global capital." He looked resignedly through the window, perhaps contemplating what was left of his life's work. "We're just going round and round in circles. To defend ourselves against the Germans we'd have to join up with the Serbs, and vice versa."

"But I'm more interested in the short-term."

"I'm not!" Olenić snapped. "I don't have time for that at my age. I know what newspapers are. If I talk to you about Rijeka Bank you'll put that in the title and throw out everything significant."

He stood there silently, weakly backlit by the light fighting through the window. This old guy came from serious times. By some miracle he was still here; perhaps he was the last of them. Old modernists. How serious they were, how focused and goal-oriented. If I met the Tito of 1937 today—if he stepped out of a time machine and into Limited and told me what he thought—I'd likely swear he was mad.

I poured myself another whiskey.

Lightning flashed outside, and he turned and looked at me. He probably considered me a drunkard. It seemed he was waiting for me to go.

But I couldn't go yet; I was short an anecdote. So I started talking in a roundabout way about Kiro Gligorov. Earlier, Olenić had pronounced his name with affection.

He sat down again. He poured himself a little whiskey too, a good sign.

"It's interesting," he mused, "for a moment there you reminded me very much of Kiro."

"You're joking."

"I was at a symposium down in Macedonia several years ago. Someone remembered me, and I was invited."

He seemed to soften, the hardness melted from his face, and he told me a tale—a remarkable tale about the collapse of Yugoslavia:

"Seeing as I was down there, I thought I should call in on Kiro. When you go to a country and know the president it's a shame not to visit him. Kiro was getting toward the end of his second term in office, so I didn't think he'd be all that busy. We were sitting in his office and his mobile phone was ringing all the time; he'd just recently received it and didn't know how to turn it off. I didn't know either.

"It was just like now when we were talking, except that his was ringing all the time. He was president, after all. But he didn't know how to turn it off, so the two of us old men sat there in front of the mobile and looked at it. It was haranguing us like a crying child.

"As his mobile was ringing, I was complaining about our pensions, and he said: 'Ole—,' he always called me that, 'you know, Ole, my pay is 700 marks, and I'm president, and I keep thinking I could have more, but it'd be unpleasant to ask them to give me a raise.'

"Kiro was always like that, you know. We had a nice long chat although his mobile was ringing all the time and annoying us. At one point he asked: 'Who should succeed me as president?' His second term in office was drawing to a close, so he couldn't run again. Now he needed to choose someone who he could personally support, but he still didn't know which of the young fellows would do.

"I said to him: 'Well, I don't know—I don't really follow things here—but what about Vasil Tupurkovski?' You know, Tupurkovski, the paunchy guy with the handlebar moustache who always wore a woolen jumper. But he wasn't stupid, and he had experience—political experience—back in Yugoslavia, and he was a socialist, so I expected he could be good.

"And Kiro said to me: 'Vasil? Yes, I'm thinking about him too. It's not that there are any who are better, but I'm really not sure.'

"Kiro thought deeply for a moment. Then he asked me: 'Do you remember, Ole, when Yugoslavia was collapsing? It was the last Party Congress.' He told me about the last session where everything went down the plughole, when first of all the Slovenians left, and then Račan and the Croatians walked out too. But before that things had gone on all blinking day, there had been one argument and quarrel after another, it was drama nonstop, the tension lasted for hours, the session dragged on into the evening and still no end was in sight. Vasil was sitting next to him and kept whispering in his ear that he was starving.

"Kiro told him: 'Wait a bit, you can see they all want to go—the Slovenians, the Croatians—and if you go now it'll look like we Macedonians were the first to leave.'

"Then, when the Slovenians had left, Vasil whispered to Kiro: 'All right, I'm going now.'

"But Kiro still wouldn't let him.

"'Come on, Kiro, I'm starving,' Vasil pleaded. But Kiro put his foot down: 'Be patient. You can see the country's falling apart. I don't want people to say that we let Yugoslavia collapse because you were hungry. Wait for the break, or else history will judge you!'

"'Fortunately the others were famished too, so they set up a smorgasbord and Vasil was able to fill up,' Kiro said. 'But I just took two canapés. I didn't feel like eating anything much, you see, because I saw what was coming. I could even count the dead—believe me, I had experience.'

"'The session was restarted after the smorgasbord but it soon finished again because neither the Slovenians nor the Croatians returned to the hall,' Kiro said.

"Now I can't remember exactly all the details he told me, but you appreciate the situation. Kiro continued: 'What could we do? So I said to Vasil: Let's go back to Skopje. We have no choice—there's nothing we can do here any more.'

"This was all quite a blow for Kiro because he'd built up Yugoslavia and seen through the reforms.

"And Kiro said: 'We got our things and went to the car, and I told the chauffeur: "To the airport!" And I thought to myself: Yugoslavia has collapsed, a historical epoch has ended; here I am now, and who knows if I'll ever come back to Belgrade; and a fine rain was falling, it made you feel despondent.'

"But Vasil disturbed him and said: 'Kiro, there's a nice little place here in Karaburma that's open all night and always has

fresh roast.' Kiro looked at him: 'Haven't you just eaten, Vasil?
I can't eat, my appetite's gone, I just feel miserable. You can go,
if you like, and I'll stay in the car and doze a bit,' Kiro said. 'We
drove there and Vasil went into the eatery, but he probably felt
awkward knowing I was waiting in the car, so he came back
ten minutes later with some slices of roast in a plastic bag.
And so we headed for the airport; I leaned my head against
the window, I wanted to calm my nerves, to doze a bit, but the
crackling of the cellophane was in my ears all the time because
he was rummaging in that bag.

"We boarded the plane and rose up above Belgrade, and I
looked out into the night. I wanted to go to sleep so much, so
I closed my eyes, but I kept thinking: What's going to happen
now? My life flashed before my eyes and I thought: Yugoslavia
has failed, I can't believe it. What's going to happen to
Macedonia now if everyone starts grabbing whatever bits they
can? So that abyss was down below us, I couldn't get to sleep,
and I kept hearing the crackle of the cellophane as he rustled
in the bag; the noise really bothered me, Ole, and I was upset;
I opened my eyes and looked at Vasil, about to tell him off, but
stopped. I just couldn't believe it all, and I watched him as he
demolished that meat.

"When he saw I was looking at him, he said: 'Kiro, there's
nothing better than cold pork chop!'

"Kiro's mobile on the table kept ringing as he was telling me
this, and I didn't know if he was getting agitated because of it
or because of the story.

"And then Kiro spread his arms and said: 'So tell me, Ole—
could he be the president?'"

That was too long for an anecdote in the newspaper, I figured
as I left Olenić's building. The rain was easing up and I was

hungry, almost like Vasil, so I retro-ed into a dank diner
left over from the previous system. I had the old waitress in
orthopedic work shoes bring me tripe soup. Usually I found
backwaters like this relaxing, but today I remembered that I
had ignored Milka's calls.

I felt that I couldn't beat around the bush with Milka. She
a mother and I just a journalist. Provincial women know their
area of operation: family and extended-family concerns. They
leave politics and other foreign affairs to the menfolk, but as
far as extended-family matters are concerned—if someone
happens to need supervising, keeping tabs on, or brainwashing,
if a confession and an expression of penitence have to be
elicited—they're on deck. I'd always known that Milka was the
informal boss of the extended-family ministry of the interior.
She went to visit everyone, called up regularly, inquired, and
interrogated. She even kept in touch with distant relatives on
other continents.

When she came to our place she always complained about
her son, and she provoked my old ma to complain about me
too. So in my presence they complained together, about my
unfinished studies, about me not yet being married, not having
children, not having a flat of my own, and guzzling beer by the
gallon. This yammering was their medium, and it devastated
everything around them. Milka very quickly made me feel
miserable even when I thought things were going wonderfully.
I was glad not to have seen Milka since she had that falling-out
with my ma. That was where the conflict began. Milka was the
elder and acted like an authority and couldn't forgive my ma
for aligning herself contrary to caucus instructions. But my old
ma persisted bravely in her mutiny.

The downside was that she had to endure the long-term
consequences. Milka had done thorough groundwork to turn
the whole extended family against my ma and make her a kind

of dissident, isolating our family from the rest of the clan. As
a consequence, my mother became embittered, as edgy as a
Soviet defector with the KGB on her heels.

Since we didn't have anything else to talk about, my mother
continually informed me about the development of the
conflict, which from here in Zagreb looked like a soap opera.
I sometimes recounted that colorful Mediterranean imbroglio
with a smile at parties. All the same, my ma carried out her
dissident struggle and it kept her alive; otherwise, life as a
pensioner would have killed her.

Yet I hadn't thought about that in depth, the way Olenić
thought about the economy. From my perspective, the whole
thing seemed unreal and unrelated to me. But thinking about
it now it was clear that my old ma had one ace up her sleeve:
me. She gave everyone my number to prove the modern power
of our faction. Perhaps we didn't have any real support on the
ground, but we held the capital and the media. The West was
on our side, and the liberal intellectuals too.

Only now did I realize what it meant that my mother
sent Boris to me. She gave him my number and sent him to
me like a misfit who scrounges a favor—as if he was seeking
asylum. She wanted it to be a public humiliation for Milka
in the eyes of the family. That was why Milka and Boris
weren't communicating. He'd accepted the help of the family
dissident and betrayed his mother—he'd gone over to the
other side like the Bolshoi Theater ballet dancer who sold his
homosexual soul.

My involvement in all of this was much deeper than I'd
realized. Milka now assumed, logically enough, that I was
part of the conspiracy. And I was. Damn it, in Milka's eyes I
was the chief operative in the service of my ma. My ma had
devised a plot, and I had put it into practice. Not only had we
humiliated Milka by driving her own son to betray her, but

we'd even gone so far as to send her son to Iraq to disappear in the desert.

Everything I'd run from for decades had caught up with me. The provincial world and all that went with it were pursuing me like a posse. The past, spirits of a pre-modern life: everything that I wanted to emancipate myself from. I imagined myself running across an urban wasteland hotly pursued by peasants armed with pitchforks and whatever they could lay their hands on, and Milka was leading them on like Delacroix's Marianne, an open-shirted heroine boldly raising her arm and advancing with her old boobs at the fore.

I'd fled to Zagreb and become a city boy; here I went to a thousand concerts, lived with an actress who played avant-garde dramas, I acted cool, and did everything right. The fear of someone thinking I was a redneck made me read totally unintelligible postmodernist books, watch unbearable avant-garde films, and listen to progressive music even when I wasn't in the mood. I was terrified of everything superficial and populist. If something became too popular, I rejected it. Even in moments of major inebriation when I felt like singing a popular peasant song I stopped myself. I maintained discipline. But in vain. All at once they were breathing down my neck again. I thought I'd given them the slip, but now they'd encircled me, having used Boris as bait, and were closing in for the kill.

Half pissed already but needing to drown these thoughts I went and stood at the bar. I tried to strike up a conversation with the waitress about the war in Iraq, purely along the lines of whether the war had been worse here or if it was worse there. Since Boris had survived here as a soldier, I wanted to assure myself that he'd probably survive there as a civilian.

The waitress calmly ignored me; she'd apparently learned in her school of bar diplomacy that one shouldn't talk about the war with fellows my age because you couldn't tell who had post-traumatic stress disorder and who had a cousin in Iraq.

I phoned Sanja; she said she was going home to relax before the premiere, so I decided to return to the office to give her some peace. There I checked my email, excited to see a message from Vito Čuveljak, the Reuters cameraman in Iraq. But he didn't know anything about Boris.

Just as I started working on the interview with Olenić, my mobile started ringing again. Milka. I switched the ringer to vibrate. Every few minutes or so my mobile trembled.

I shouldn't have sent him there. That's all I can say to her. What else can I do?

But I didn't answer.

My mother called. She'd read Sanja's interview. "I'm ashamed she's talking about sex like that."

"She talks about it—and you're ashamed?"

"I'm ashamed."

"What did she say to get you so hot?"

"Hot? Why canna' ya talk like a normal human being? If ya don' mind. Whaddid she say? She said she'd go naked for a film. Insteada gettin' married and havin' kids, she'd go naked for a film! Y'are not normal."

"That's just how it is."

"Is that all you have to say?"

"I'm at work. I can't talk now."

"I dunno where you're from, and who made you and brought you up. I dunno why you've turned out the way you are."

Next, Markatović called. His voice was subdued.

He was calling from the bathroom; his wife was packing suitcases.

"Whose suitcases?" I asked.

"Hers. When someone's going away they pack their own suitcases."

"Where's she going?"

"I don't know," he whispered. "She's gone crazy."

"What happened?"

"I told her I had shares in Rijeka Bank and was still waiting to see what happened."

"Where's she going?"

"I said I don't know."

"Well, ask her, man."

"But she's crazy."

"So what?"

"All right. I'll go and ask her," Markatović muttered and hung up.

In the end Sanja rang too. She said she'd been napping and had been woken by the phone—or rather by Milka. She didn't believe I wasn't there. And when Sanja asked her politely to leave her in peace because she had a play, Milka replied that she would also like to have a play with us because we had it coming, so Sanja unplugged the phone and did a bit of meditation. Now she felt better. She was just about to leave for the theater and suggested we meet after the premiere. I wished her good luck and said everything would be just fine.

I called Markatović and said, "My head hurts."

"Why are you telling me?"

"Because I'm going to switch off my mobile, take one of those popular tablets, and go home for a bit of a kip. Just so you don't think I'm trying to avoid you while your drama is going on."

He mumbled absently.

"What's happened? Is Dijana still there?"

"She's locked herself in the bedroom. I looked through the keyhole. She's writing. I guess she's writing me a letter."

"Call me when you get it."

Tits.

Darkness.

The end.

She'd done it. The palms of my hands were moist.

The applause was thunderous.

It's rare to hear any critical opinions in the lobby after a play. But half an hour later, when the first discussions were taking place over drinks and canapés, things started to look different.

There are people whose mission it is to be the first to pass negative judgment. These are people who attend all cultural events, although they don't like anything. Charly was one of them. I saw him coming up to me with an enigmatic smile as if to remind me that I was one of them too.

"The director botched things up a bit," he said.

Charly had always wanted to study stage direction. "I wouldn't have said so," I replied.

"The actors are good but the director messed things up," he pressed.

"And how was Sanja?"

"Excellent. But, really, you have to admit, the director messed things up a bit."

Just then Ela appeared. Charly went all stiff as if he'd been jabbed with a needle. She nodded to Charly and gave me a kiss on each cheek. "Sanja was just phenomenal," she gushed.

"And how are you?" she asked Charly in a gentle, almost maternal way.

A glance behind them showed Silva coming—complications

were in store. I said I had to go to the toilet and disappeared before Charly could do anything about it.

I waited at the bar until Sanja came. She hadn't changed. That cheap costume really was sexy. I'd put on the suit I wear to weddings and funerals. I kissed her. She grabbed my ass, and I automatically looked around to see if anyone was watching.

"Look at you in that suit," she said.

"Well, I thought I had to."

"But it's dashing."

People around the bar looked at us. They had lots of reasons to look at us, but I got the impression it was mostly her butt in that white, vinyl miniskirt. Her belly button was showing beneath the blouse sewn together with the white push-up bra that enlarged her breasts. The little white glitter boots and the white cowboy hat made her look like the ultimate lady of the night. Even I couldn't resist looking at her tits instead of her eyes.

"You were great," I whispered in her ear. "You really turn me on."

"You too," she whispered back.

She seemed more flirtatious than usual. "Are you on something?" I asked.

"Doc brought some coke. We've just had a snort. Wanna leave this crowd?"

I followed her through the people. She stopped in front of the men's bathroom.

"Check if anyone's in there."

I peeked in. A guy was washing his hands. When he left, we dashed inside. There was just one stall amidst the urinals. We went into the cubicle and locked the door.

I kissed her and grabbed her hard by the ass. I felt I was about to explode. She lowered the toilet lid, sat on it and started to unbutton my pants. My dick bounced out. She looked me in the eyes from below, shook her head with a grin, and then took me in her mouth.

Her hat blocked my view of the action, so I took it off her and put it on my head. She let my dick out of her mouth for a second and in a mock naive voice said, "Are you some kind of cowboy?"

"Yeah, just passin' through."

The door squeaked. Someone started using one of the urinals. Sanja went back to sucking. I was terrified. The door squeaked again, and this time someone rattled the stall handle. I almost stopped breathing. Sanja licked me wickedly from below.

"And what do you say about the acting?" a voice muttered at the urinals. It sounded like Doc.

"She's got a good pair of tits," was the response.

That piece of theater critique in the men's room obviously amused Sanja, and she nodded and made some grunts of consent as she was sucking away.

She's mad, I thought, in a panic that in no way lessened my excitement. The coke had an interesting effect on her. The men were still talking. I fought off my orgasm but she didn't stop, and I watched as she changed rhythm, without any sign of relenting; she took it deep, and mumbled quietly, which they probably didn't hear out there, I hoped, but I wasn't worrying about that any more because the situation obviously turned her on even more. I wouldn't be able to hold on anyway. Yes, that was obvious, and now I shuddered as I came. She waited until the end, and then smiled up at me. I kissed her hair.

"OK then, let's go," she whispered when she heard the door slam.

Out in the corridor I saw Doc who'd stopped to talk to a girl, and he called out to us, "What are you up to here?"

"Just having a blow," Sanja said in a shrill voice, pretending to be a bad fairy.

Doc burst out laughing. He was wearing a garish orange T-shirt with ANTI-DRUGS HOTLINE printed on it.

We headed toward the lobby.

At the abundant buffet, I helped myself to some white wine, had a few sips, and reached for a canapé with a lettuce leaf and a little turd on top; at least that's what it looked like, but it tasted OK.

Suddenly, a flash went off in my face and Sanja was grabbing my arm. She'd been looking into the flash and didn't notice that my mouth was full. I dodged her. By the time I finally swallowed that blasted canapé, Sanja was surrounded by journalists, flashes going off all around her. I considered rejoining her but didn't want to be seen as the star's boyfriend desperate to emerge from his anonymity.

I drank my wine and thought about how I'd have to cut out her photos when they came out in the papers so when she became a big star and left me, I'd always be able to look at the photos, those eyes, that smile, that mouth that still had my semen in it, and be able to wank over those photos.

The thought exhilarated me in a perverse way at first, but then I rejected it as depressing. She wasn't going to leave me. Where did I get that idea? This isn't Hollywood, I consoled myself. I was relieved when Sanja reappeared and kissed me. More flashes. I couldn't believe this was really happening to us.

It always showed when guys were unable to live with the success of their wives. I'd seen guys lose their alpha roles and was sure it wouldn't happen to me if Sanja made it big. But right there and then, at the very first step, I began to feel inferior. Was I really such a redneck?

Had she anticipated all this? Was the blowjob just

compensation? No, I told myself: it was proof that nothing would change. It was proof because she also needed it. Standing there in the white hat beside Sanja, the flashes fired at me, and I laughed at the way fame—even a tiny brush with it—accelerates your thoughts and opens up a new space in front of you, in which you can easily become lost.

I drank my wine too quickly and my glass was empty so I looked around to see how to get hold of another as fast as possible. Ela probably had the same problem, and we found ourselves at the table at the same time. We each took another glass.

"Hasn't Sanja seen you?" I asked.

"You can see what bedlam there is," she said. "There'll be time."

"How are things otherwise?"

"Fantastic."

Fantastic, fantastic, fantastic, uh-huh, I thought. What are we going to talk about now? Should I say everything's fantastic too and we wind down the show?

"And you?" she asked.

"Disaster."

"You're kidding? What's happened?"

"Oh come on, Ela, we're allowed to be fucked up—it's not a crime."

"What are you getting at?"

"You and I don't have to get into that super-cool bullshit. We've known each other from back when I didn't have a washing machine."

Fortunately that made her laugh. Then Sanja came over to us. She and Ela kissed and exchanged a few lines of small talk, almost at a scream. But I could see that, after the initial enthusiasm, Sanja was at a bit of a loss with her. She was simply in a much more lively frame of mind than poor Ela, who'd probably given up drugs and everything else fun because she was too busy dieting.

I wanted to leave the two of them before Sanja scampered off again leaving me alone with Ela. I didn't want to be standing there with her like two outsiders. I glanced at Sanja and it seemed she was looking right through us.

Then Jerman turned up. We'd been inseparable during our Drama days at uni. I congratulated him on his performance, but I felt strangely tense seeing him there, that headline OUR CHEMISTRY HAPPENED ON STAGE going round and round in my head.

"Let's go and have a drink," he said.

"You can see we're drinking already," I said.

"But there's no beer here. I'm going to the bar for a beer."

"He's all over the place," Ela laughed.

"As mad as a cabbage," Sanja said.

I stood there as if in the midst of opposing forces.

"I'm going out for some fresh air," I said.

"Are you not feeling well?" Sanja was startled.

"No, everything's fine."

I gave back her hat.

"You're sure you're OK?"

"It's just a bit stuffy."

Just air, an ordinary Zagreb night, the sound of cars from the main road, kids rushing to the tram stop because they'd overshot their curfews. I needed some unpretentious damp pavement and the couple who shared a hot dog at the fast food stall and were taking bites in turn.

I looked at all this like someone who was sheltering from the rain, standing close to the tram stop, by a shop window with a mass of trendy sneakers.

I kept walking on along the street, aimlessly, till I reached the main square. Then I felt lost, like someone who'd dropped

out of their own story, so I started to head back down a
different street, through Flower Square, and gradually I got
myself together, as if I'd inhaled a dose of intimacy in those
streets.

When I got back I finally took the infamous cocaine from
my pocket.

"So that's why you had to go out for some fresh air," Sanja
exclaimed.

I rounded up Charly and Silva. I also found Ela, who
daintily declined, but came with us since Charly was there.
Sanja took us backstage to a rehearsal room in the maze of
corridors beneath the theater. After snorting a few lines we
returned through the labyrinth like a squad ready for action
and burst onto the small stage that had been made into an
improvised disco. Some guy was already there, dancing—
Markatović!

His tie flapped and he danced as if he was shaking off a dog
that had bitten his leg. Silva and Sanja joined in with some
sexy dance, Ela began to meditatively move her hips and neck,
and Charly sort of hopped around mechanically and waved his
arms in some arrhythmic techno style. I raised my arms like a
footballer who'd just scored a goal and grinned at Markatović.

I screamed in his ear, "What happened with Dijana?"

"You won't understand," Markatović shrilled in a broken
voice. "You just won't understand."

Afterward he told me in a voice dripping with
sentimentality that he'd come because of Sanja and me. He was
so glad we were happy.

The party was hotting up.

People were circulating through the foyer between the bar
and the dance floor that had taken over the stage. Every hour

or so we went down into the labyrinth of corridors, and the conversations became ever more candid and stupid.

Markatović explained to me that Sanja and I were a perfect couple. He spoke of her as a sophisticated lady, at whose side my life would never become languid, while claiming in a devastated voice that Dijana had become a domestic bore. What did he expect when she was freighted with twins, I tried telling him.

But he wouldn't listen: he said she was becoming more and more like her mother, and that horrified him because he hadn't imagined life would be like this, what with loans and all that shit, with Dolina and bad shares on his back, and a wife who reminded him of his mother-in-law. He added that after the birth she'd even stopped enjoying sex—they'd had to cut her down there and now it hurt. He told me all this although I hadn't asked. But he confessed to me in a terribly trusting tone and with the face of a drowning man. Dijana had left, taken the twins with her, and written a fourteen-page farewell letter, but he hadn't got round to reading it yet because he had come here because he knew I'd be here.

Next, Silva came up to me and whispered that the Chief hadn't been enthusiastic about her taking on the Niko Brkić topic; he'd told her to stick to covering showbiz because that was what she did best. She leaned her head on my shoulder and worried sadly that everyone considered her empty-headed. I told her she wasn't. I looked around to see if this was going to make Sanja jealous, but she was dancing with her back to me. Ela was pressing Charly against the wall, writhing sensually in front of him, and he seemed to be gradually giving in to the pressure.

Charly came up to me a bit later. "Where'd Silva get to?"

"She left," I said.

He stayed beside me, pensive and fumbling around on his mobile. Someone had put on a remixed domestic folk song; Charly made an expression of disgust. Markatović, on the other hand, raised his arms, dancing recklessly.

"What am I, what are you, oh liiife," he bellowed.

"Your friend seems a little unhappy," Charly remarked, as if he didn't know Markatović's name.

He wasn't the only one, I thought. But we were careful not to admit it. That was one of the codes of Zagreb society. We were pretty disciplined about that. I guess we felt that distinguished us from the hoi polloi of the Balkans.

"What am I, what are you, oh liiife," Markatović continued— it must have been cathartic. He grabbed a bottle of water from a table and started pouring it over his head. A circle of people formed around him. Sanja and Ela were there too, killing themselves with laughter. Markatović's face beamed with happiness.

"A system meltdown," I said to Charly with a grin.

"Is this a Croatian theater or are we in some bloody Serbian wedding?" Charly jeered.

"It doesn't matter," I said. "They're letting it all hang out."

"I can't stand it. You think this is all OK?"

"It's all a laugh, one big laugh."

"I don't get you one fucking bit."

Again that ontologically naive refrain blared: *What am I, what are you, oh liiife*. If it had been sung by Irish folk musicians Charly would relate to it more favorably.

"Translate the lyrics into English and then it won't bother you so much," I said.

"That's just bullshit, and you know it."

"You're maintaining discipline, at three in the morning?"

He was offended. That's what we're like in Croatia when the fun starts. We try to make sure things don't get out of control.

There's always that danger here on the slippery edge of the Balkans. Here we always squabble about what we're allowed to enjoy and what not. That was part of our culture. We had high standards in order to set ourselves apart from the primitives further south and east. We were small in number, those of us who held high standards, and were aware of our precarious position. Until we collapsed like Markatović.

Now I was angry too. Charly had dragged me into this shitty debate and, in a typical Central European way, I started to think instead of having fun. But the coke rocketed me to be brutally honest.

"You know what?" I began. "I've been wanting to tell you for ages that your standards are utterly destructive. And you've come here in such a shitty mood just because of Ela."

"What the hell. What's she got to do with it?"

"She's hot on you, but you can't. Your stupid fucking high standards are in the way because you've got your sights on Silva. You keep on trying to meet some artificial standard, you drive around in that fat Jaguar, you go on about locally-grown olive oil, but you don't fool anyone. I'm smashed and I don't care, but I'm telling you. Get rid of those fucking fictions. Bloody hell, I can see where you're at. You don't have a life. You're always into imitations. You think people don't see? Just let people dance, man, go over to Ela and pour water over your head. Otherwise your life will just be one big put-on."

"It's about time I put on something," Doc said as he walked past us.

"Go ahead!" I called out after him. "People here are about to take to the barricades."

"Don't you think I can see where you're at?" Charly retaliated. He'd consumed quite a bit of coke himself, and his eyes glared with self-assurance as he stared at me like in a pre-election debate on TV. "You'd like to run with the hare and hunt with the hounds. You let it hang out at the paper as if you're so cool, kind of, like you don't push in anywhere. In fact, you're not allowed to show ambition because it'd sorta look like you weren't a punk. You've listened to too many smash-the-system songs and read too many books about underdogs. But now you're packing shit. Your girlfriend's made it big and now you have to do something too. Isn't that right? So just be honest with yourself. You've been part of the system for ages. Otherwise your life, like you said, will just be one big put-on."

> *Stop the war in the name of love*
> *Stop the war in the name of God*
> *Stop the war in the name of children*
> *Stop the war in Croatia.*
> *Let Croatia be one of Europe's stars*
> *Europe, you can stop the war.*

That was the song that Doc had put on.
"He's mad," Charly said.
"What, you don't like this either?"

"Are you cool?" Sanja asked.
"Cool and hot," I said. "I'm happy because of you!"
I kissed her and grabbed her ass, but she moved away, saying, "Careful. There might still be photojournalists around."
"So what? We're a couple."
"No, come on, it'd look nasty."
"You know, I could perhaps get a regular column."
"That's fantastic."
"I just negotiated it today: The Red Bull Generation."
"What's that?"
"Life, fervor, taking things to the limits."

"Fantastic, fantastic," she said, kissing me before moving back to the dance floor.

Markatović was walking with difficulty. Suffering heavy casualties. Now he stood in front of me. "I love people, but not too much."

I laughed.

"I'm going to the loo. Are you staying here?"

"Sure, I'm not going anywhere in a hurry."

Then Jerman came shuffling along.

"Shall we go and have a drink?"

"Sure."

We went through the lobby to the bar.

"Hey, y'know, what was in the paper, fucking hell. It doesn't have the slightest bit to do with reality, y'know?"

"I know."

"I just wanna say it so you know."

"It's not worth a mention. I get you."

"OK, what are you having?" He ordered, and then introduced me to Ingo.

Ingo Grinschgl. The director. An East German and, worst of all, he looked like an East German. His pock-marked face and hippie hairstyle told us he wasn't a Westerner who'd show us the meaning of trendy. A bearded German who learned from Jerman and Doc not to believe anyone in the Balkans.

He praised Sanja: "She hez a greyt fyutcha." He was drunk but still a bit too serious, very polite and way outside the whole vibrant social scene. The language barrier hampered him. Besides, no one could stick to a single topic at this time of night. He looked like he was watching things flying past as I told him about my job.

"Here I am!" I called out to Markatović who was looking around where he'd left me. I said to Ingo, "Mai frend, lost in speis."

"Wot you sey abaut ze ekonomik situeyshen hier?" asked Ingo.

"Oh, itts too difikult to ekspleyn."

"What are you mumbling?" Markatović butted in.

"I'm speaking English and explaining the economic situation to this German."

"It's a disaster," Markatović said. He made the most passionate of expressions and got very close to Ingo. "A DI-SA-STER!"

Ingo nodded with sympathy. "Thet's terribl."

"Jermans. Deutsch, you undrstand? Deutsch peepl buy benk. My benk," Markatović said, simplifying things somewhat. "And naw, dizasta! Nix benk! Kaine gelt! KA-TA-STRO-FA!"

"It was like this," Doc began. "A girl came up to me. She was from one of those socially deprived areas, it doesn't matter exactly where, but I wanna make the point that she was from one of those areas because this is a social story. And y'know, her dad was a civil servant there, so he arranged for her to be given a nice scholarship, although she wasn't such a great student. Her dad pulled all the strings via the party to have her enrolled at uni, in Medicine, because in those areas, y'know, every woman who goes to the hairdresser's dreams of her child becoming a doctor and treating her. Anyway, the girl had seen me in some commercial. I was at The Blitz and she came up to bum a cigarette. She had no idea I was an actor, she'd just seen me in a window ad, and really liked me. Anyway, Jeezus, we screwed all night long, fucking hell. And that was that. I mean, I didn't promise her the moon, kinda that we'd I don't know what, though she sure was cute. No gift of the gab but she had good tits and was a maniac, so saucy, giving back all she learned down there in the socially deprived area. And y'know what? She left in the morning, went straight to uni and I never saw her again. And no, I'm not finished.

"They had microscope practice up at the Medical School that morning. I heard all this from one of her girlfriends who'd been there that night at The Blitz. I ran into her just yesterday and she told me the story, though it all happened back in the autumn. So this friend of the country girl told me they'd had microscope practice and that everyone had a look at their own saliva under the microscope and everyone saw some kind of micro-organisms, only my girl saw something special. She called her friend over—the one who told me the story, and she looked and saw something pretty damn big. My girl called out: 'Professor, professor, come and see this!' The professor came over and looked and said, 'Miss, those things in your saliva are nothing out of the ordinary, just spermatozoa.' Talk about embarrassing!

"But what happened afterward was pretty fateful. Tragic. This is what her friend told me: she stopped going to uni and, of course, hit drugs straight away—heroin first thing, zoom—and when her folks found out they made her go home, back down south. That was the collapse of all the family's expectations, the end of their hopes, and the beginning of a big family mess. Her old man went round the bend and killed his old woman, shot her, he probably wanted to kill the girl but hit his old woman, the cops aren't really sure, but the main thing is that he's now in custody, and the girl has run away and no one knows where she is. I feel a bit guilty about it. Sounds like a novel, dunnit? It could be a real hit—it's got sex, blood, and it's a social story too."

"Doc, you're repulsive," Sanja gave him a look of disgust.

"I knew I'd end up being the culprit!"

We'd all gathered behind the bar. They'd turned the music off too. The best time for the worst stories.

Sanja continued. "I didn't think sperm could survive."

"It's all bullshit, you just made it all up," Markatović laughed at Doc raucously.

"He's revolting," I chipped in, glancing at Doc.

"Like bloody hell I made it up!" Doc snorted righteously. "Who'd invent a story like that?"

"Coud you trensleyt it?" Ingo asked.

"Itts too difikult," I said.

"It woz my luv stori. Veri difikult," Doc added.

DAY FOUR

The phone rang and rang.

"Go and see what's up," Sanja whined, butting me with her elbow.

I opened my eyes. A glance at the clock: seven thirty in the morning. It was Milka, it couldn't have been anyone else.

"It's nothing—it'll stop," I whispered.

And sure enough, it rang and rang a bit more and then stopped.

I sank back into sleep but the phone blared again. As chief of the family police, Milka obviously knew that you can soften up a prisoner with sleep deprivation.

"Unplug it, please," Sanja pleaded, a collateral victim.

I had to get up to reach the phone and I was still smashed from the night before. I banged into the doorpost with a real kerthump and fell, knocking over the books and newspapers piled on the plastic box where I kept important documents.

"Jeezus," she said, getting out of bed and crouching down next to me. "Are you OK?"

The phone and the whole world around me now rang even louder. Since Sanja had got up too and I was wussing out about Milka, I implored her, "Go and see who it is."

Sanja tottered to the phone.

"Say I'm not here!" I yelled.

I collapsed back to bed. I just needed to gather strength and then I'd make a dent in the day. But Sanja yelled from the living room. "Toni, your editor wants you."

Pero, at seven thirty?

"Come to the office immediately," he commanded.

"Why, what's wrong?"

"Cut the blathering and get a move on."

"He's not exactly in a good mood," I told Sanja when I returned to the room, which reeked of alcohol.

"I dreamed I was examining a tortoise," she said.

"What?"

"It kept pulling in its head, arms, and legs. What does that mean?"

"Tortoises don't have arms," I stated mechanically.

"Yes they do!" she said.

I put some water for Nescafé in the microwave, and my head spun with drunken premonitions that made my hands shake. I figured that I'd had about one hour's sleep.

Sanja called out from the bedroom. "Have a look if there's anything in the papers about the premiere and give me a ring. I don't mind if you wake me."

Her voice was full of hope. Somehow that got to me. I felt we didn't live in the same world anymore. I had nothing to hope for. "OK," I called back. I felt like a badger from a hole. I was inside it with those drunken premonitions, and it smelled of soil, dark and earthy. Man, am I sloshed, I thought. Have a coffee! Light up a cigarette! Be the man you were!

I hurried into the Chief's office. He and Secretary were sitting there. Secretary looked at me without a word, and the Chief's gaze searched the ceiling and walls as if he was tracking a mosquito he intended to kill.

"Good morning," I offered.

"Good morning?" the Chief asked. "Brilliant morning, I'd say."

He stood up, lifted the newspaper from the table like a matador and held it right in front of my nose, so close that I couldn't read it.

"Careful, it's still hot," the Chief said.

It was GEP's weekly *Monitor*, and the bold letters of the title page blared out: CROATIAN REPORTER MISSING IN IRAQ.

"Sit down!" the Chief ordered.

I sat down.

"You don't know anything about this," the Chief said sarcastically.

"I haven't read it. You've hauled me out of bed."

Secretary nodded self-importantly, looking at my shoes.

"They exploit every opportunity," Secretary said, referring to GEP. "They'll stop at nothing. They know no limits."

I reached out for the paper but Pero whipped it away from me and, holding it in his hand, started to saunter between his table and the window.

"What absolute scum," I said, trying to channel emotion at GEP until I came up with a strategy of my own. That sometimes worked when talking about the Serbs, who you could always use for a change of focus. "Where else in Europe would this happen?"

"Do you know, perchance, which reporter they could mean here on the front page?" the Chief asked.

"I have no idea which reporter this is about, but . . ."

"But what?" the Chief said and lit up a cigarette, reminding me of the Gestapo interrogator in a Yugoslav partisan film. I cast myself as the good guy.

"But since you've called me in, it could obviously be our fellow in Iraq."

"Obviously, huh?"

"Theoretically it could be him."

"Well, why weren't you at least decent to that woman?"

"Which woman?"

"With the mother of our reporter!"

Unbelievable—bloody Milka had done me in. And so quickly?

How did an idler like Boris end up on the front page? Since when was he so important?

The Chief waved the paper.

CROATIAN REPORTER MISSING IN IRAQ.

After the attack on the World Trade Center our papers came out with title pages saying how many Croatians had died. We searched for them. If none of our people had been in the Twin Towers we would've been disappointed. We so much wanted to be part of world news. We elbowed our way into it with the same zeal as Icho Kamera when he elbowed his way into the scene at car accidents. And this thing with Boris now on the cover, you had to admit, was the logical extension. If he'd disappeared anywhere else he could just rot. But there we had it: a Croatian reporter had disappeared in the great vortex of Iraq. Was this the first Croatian victim in Iraq?

"Are you in your right mind?" the Chief asked.

"It's a fake," I said analytically. "They're after the first Croatian victim in Iraq. It's kinda like the wow-we're-participating-in-the-global-drama discourse, don't you see?"

The Chief looked at me dully, but I continued. "Man, if we got drawn into that war they'd break out the champers."

"Stop going on about that," the Chief snarled. "Why didn't you call that woman?"

"My battery died."

The Chief let out a subdued moan, narrowed his eyes, and clenched his fist. Secretary looked incredibly uncomfortable.

"She's mad," I said. "I talked with her the day before yesterday and everything was normal. But yesterday my battery was low."

The Chief opened up the *Monitor*. I still didn't know what it said inside, and that significantly hindered my defense. He read aloud the passage about the "unfeeling PEG editor" who'd sent an inexperienced reporter to Iraq and then "didn't phone the reporter's worried mother for days."

"For days?" I protested. "It was just yesterday!"

"Wait for this," Pero shouted, raising his finger and continuing to read. "'When she finally managed to contact him, *Objective*'s editor even snapped at her that he had more important things to do than to talk with her about her son.'"

"I did not."

The Chief kept reading. "'It became clear to her that something had happened to her son because he hadn't phoned home for a whole week.'"

He lifted his eyes and stared at me.

"He didn't phone home at all," I said.

"Not at all?"

"That's what she told me," I said.

"All right, so why don't I know that?"

"Hang on, do you mean I'm supposed to bother you, the editor in chief," I said, "with a pissy little detail like whether or not a journalist talks with his mother? It's obvious why he's not phoning his mother—he ran all the way to Iraq to get away from her."

"Let's just take it niiice and slow."

He took to the paper again and read on. The reporter's mother was told he didn't have a satellite phone in Iraq, but the writer of the article doubted that: "To send an inexperienced fellow into the hell of war without even standard equipment—not even PEG would stoop that low." The GEP hack concluded from all this: "There's much to suggest that PEG is concealing something. Unfortunately, the anxiety of the correspondent's mother could well prove to be justified. Now it's up to PEG to come out with the whole truth."

The Chief fumed. "In this particular case, PEG means you!"

"This is all crazy. She's crazy. They're crazy."

"I don't know who's crazy here," he mused, watching me suggestively. "But I do know whose side the public is going to be on. Man, is there anything worse than a bereaved mother?"

He glanced at Secretary, hoping he'd confirm that.

I also looked at Secretary. My brain suddenly started to function like a sewing machine and I finally remembered that I'd told him yesterday I had a few problems with Boris.

I waited for him to look up at me, not just at my shoes. But his eyes returned to the Chief.

"Secretary?" I said and looked at him, waiting.

Finally he sent me a quick glance of sympathy. He had the expression of a defense witness cornered by the prosecutor's questions. The worst thing that can happen to you in life is to have a phony advocate defend you.

"You know I mentioned this to you yesterday," I said to Secretary. "But that was a mistake. I should've told the Chief." I then looked at the Chief. "A false assessment. It was my fault and I don't deny it."

"You didn't mention a thing, boy!" Secretary said, standing

up demonstratively in protest. "Who do you think you are?"

I sent him a sad glance and spelled it out. "I told you yesterday that I had a few problems with the fellow in Iraq."

Secretary went red in the face. "He's lying."

"Stop it, both of you," the Chief hissed, looking slightly disoriented.

"I'm really thirsty," I said. "Last night we stayed on after the premiere."

The Chief's eyes sought the ceiling and he spread his arms as if addressing the gods who were so unkind. "Go and get some water then."

I went into the corridor where there was a water cooler with cold, pure spring water. I carried two plastic cups back to the office, put them on the table and sat down. I didn't look at Secretary at all.

The Chief had now decided to take a slightly more humane stance toward me. "Tell me everything. Why did his mom make you panic like that?"

"That woman . . . Milka. It's hard to explain."

"The guy had a piece in the last issue. But his mom must've caught on, via you, that something was wrong. Correct?"

"Yes."

"What a balls-up! See what you've done? You blew her off, and she called the competitors to take revenge. A right bloody mess. So it's not she who's crazy. Neither are they crazy. Because it's not just about her having called them. No! Because, check this: they poked around and figured out that you sent emails to people in Iraq asking around about our reporter. Do you know what I'm talking about?"

"I do," I said. There was no way out anymore.

"I don't want to waste any more time," the Chief said. "Tell me what the hell is going on."

I scratched the back of my head. Should I start with the big bang between Milka and my old ma and finish with the war in Iraq?

"It's all terribly complicated. He never got in touch by phone, only ever by email. Now it's four days since his last email. I got a bit worried, but if you look at it rationally there needn't be any reason to panic. He doesn't have to get in touch every day."

All at once the Chief spoke to me intimately, like a friendly copper. "Look, I'm not accusing you. If you said that to Secretary . . ."

But Secretary immediately got up again and stood right in front of me. "You haven't got an ounce of integrity. Imagine behaving like that toward a mother who's searching for her son, when the man's in the middle of a war! That says everything about you."

It was incredible: Milka's words still found their mark when they came at me secondhand.

"I can't talk with him," I complained.

"Secretary," the Chief said, "if you can't help me, then at least leave me to work in peace."

Secretary was hyperventilating like a heart patient, his face turning an unhealthy shade of red. I thought of offering him some water, but I feared he might take that as provocation.

"I have to go for a walk," he mumbled and took his coat.

The door closed behind him.

"And?" asked the Chief.

"If I'd kicked up a panic nothing would've changed. Who'd go and search for him in Iraq? The Americans?"

"Hang on, are you now admitting he's disappeared?"

It became clear to me that we were on the same side, in a way. Neither he nor I wanted to believe Boris had disappeared.

"He hasn't disappeared, but, he's offended. I wanted to

bring him back from Iraq straight away, but he acted crazy. He pretended not to have got my messages and calls. I told him off in an email and since then he hasn't got back to me."

"Why did you keep this to yourself?"

"I covered the idiot. But what use would it've been? If he didn't listen to me he wouldn't have listened to you either."

Pero fell silent.

"Have you got any confirmation in your computer that he was in touch four days ago?"

We left his office and went to my desk.

"Here—this is his last email."

I printed it. Pero sat at Charly's desk and read.

All those desks, keyboards, phones, and large windows. There were just the two of us in the office and the space looked unusually tranquil, like the calm in the aftermath of a natural disaster. It was a damp, pastel morning. The occasional drop of rain tapped the window. Inside the air was still with the scent of fresh paper.

Down below by the intersection, a huge billboard sported a poster for a Hyundai Getz, with no down payment, in lots of installments. I followed events via that billboard: before that there'd been an ad for the Raiffeisenbank building society. There'd been the little Renault Twingo, with no down payment, in lots of installments. Tudjman had leered down at us with a bow tie. There'd been Sunmix sun cream, Lisca lingerie, and hot young flesh.

From: Boris <boris@peg.hr>
To: Toni <toni@peg.hr>

Now, folks, the war is practically over, there's
no Saddam anymore, he's vanished into thin air,
disappeared, it's like a gap in the story, a sudden draft
blowing through it, close the window will you, and if
anyone knows whether he's alive or dead they should
put up their hand, let them report it to the police. OK,
there's still no police here in Baghdad, and as long as
there's no police there's no reality. You don't know
where the borders are and what's real, I don't know if
you've noticed that it's precisely the police who make
life real, they're the mother of realism, and if there was
no realism there wouldn't be those who've skedaddled
and who we nab just to make sure they haven't left us
entirely and aren't lost to the world like Saddam, me,
or you.
Just think, folks, if there were no police there'd be no
reality and we wouldn't be able to think about it. But
now we can think because there are police, at least we
have them, but if there were no police you could do
anything that came into your head and then nothing
would be real and nothing would be legal anymore. It
would be like a neverending sentence and you'd look
in vain for a full stop or an ending, ask God, ask the
Law, ask the Next Policeman, and so on, until you run
into someone who bashes you on the head, you don't
know where the end is, how far you can really go,
what's fantasy, what's a forbidden desire, madness and
sexual imaginings, you've got no idea where you are
until you run into the next policeman and ask him, you
say you're lost, you tell him your address, and then he
takes you home to your parents, because they work
hand in glove on creating reality, they draw the edge
of the world. Who says the world has no edge? Never

mind that it's round, there has to be an edge of the
world, otherwise there's no full stop, only commas, so
you walk and walk and walk without end until you can
ask a policeman, you go bananas if you can't find him,
you look for that policeman around the world, you pray
to God that you might find him, you search like mad
for someone to arrest you and draw a line because
this is unbearable, this is unreal, can you feel that too,
please, call someone to arrest me and put me in the
nick—doesn't that sound nice—because here there's
no one competent, here there's no police, no reality,
people greet the liberators, rejoicing and spontaneous
plundering are the order of the day, people shout
"Saddam is dead" and "This is freedom," and everyone
takes something from the abandoned government
buildings and shops, seizing food, clothing, electrical
equipment, and carpets, but also Iraqi army vehicles,
computers, and even furniture from the government
offices, some remembered the museums, and people
of taste carry away works of art instead of fridges.
That's the difference in education, we were surprised
that resistance was so weak, the Yanks say, but the
resistance to reality is sometimes weak, we know that
pretty well, don't we? Although you pretend you're
a realist, deep down you were waiting for liberation
just like me, you waited for your Yanks, and they
came, you remember, recently we rejoiced like Iraqi
people. Fuck life without freedom. You know how it is
when you get carried away by a sea change, people
destroy monuments, it's an earthquake plus tsunami,
the regime is gone forever, the Yanks don't interfere
while the people are celebrating, they have exact,
predetermined tasks, they found a suicide bomber's
weapons trove in a high school, C4 explosive vests
weighing ten kilos with wires hanging out, residents
brought the Marines dozens of grenades, rockets,
and mortars from other places, the population's now
one hundred percent certain that the regime won't

be coming back, they go to the Yanks and inform on
their enemies, thinking this will help install a new
reality, informing on members of the regime who are
leftover from the former reality, but the Yanks know
exactly what they're doing, the marines are not here
to install reality, they just patrol around, bounding off
the ground like astronauts. The Iraqis no longer hold
up white flags but T-shirts, they've even begun to bare
their torsos to correspondents to assure us they're not
carrying explosives, I look at their bare torsos, state TV
is still dead, there's no picture, nothing on the screen,
that's that, remember that image, there's no image,
that's just that, Iraqi radio is still broadcasting patriotic
songs, but that's unreal, though on the other hand
nothing's real, everything is on the road, in transition,
constant improvisation, there's chaos in the city, chaos
in your head, you ought to bring the young anarchists
here to learn the trade, they're all good little children,
they're just decoration for the police as long as reality
functions. Days go by before I finish a sentence,
there's no full stop, I smoke cigarette after cigarette,
Baghdad is burning, parts of the Old Town, parts of
the best-known old street Rashid are in flames, the old
buildings are made of wood, there's no fire brigade,
as we know they died in the World Trade Center, the
fire spreads unchecked, we moved toward the German
embassy where a group of people had just begun
loading stolen goods into trucks and cars, they chased
us off, that was the very first time the locals were
unfriendly to us, but people change from hour to hour
when the revolution begins, these are fundamental
changes, the personality surges beyond its bounds, it
seethes up, color and shape melt, fear evaporates, the
worst guys are the first to feel freedom, they take in
its grandeur, freedom is an endless field, the predators
sniff it out first (first come first served!), the longer the
sentence lasts, the less kind people are. The Olympic
Hospital was looted, groups of plunderers are cruising

the city in trucks, they've begun to carry weapons
and threaten journalists who dare to take photos
of them, animals come out of the flats, vampires
out of the graves, old mummies are unravelled, the
Archaeological Museum in Baghdad, eight millennia
of Mesopotamia, has been plundered, and the exhibits
that were too heavy to be stolen were destroyed,
ambulance doctors go on their calls armed with
pistols to defend themselves against the heroes who
try to steal the vehicle and its instruments, the street
gangs size me up, I sorely miss my weapons, send me
a shipment, greet the old smugglers, congratulate
them on their deserved victory, salute those who
quietly implode. Demonstrations began down in
front of the hotel, ordinary citizens gather around
the American APCs in front of the hotel driveway
advocating repression, a middle-aged high-school
teacher called Samir, who now sells Marlboros without
tax stamps, explains to a Marine that order needs to be
restored bullet-in-the-head-wise so no one will plunder
anymore, full stop, but comma, the marine looked at
him in astonishment, and then colon, a group of Iraqi
policemen offered their services to the US forces'
Command in Baghdad—to put an end to anarchy, as
the leader of the group, Colonel Ahmed Abderazak
Said, is reported as stating on Al Jazeera . . .

"What is this?" the Chief asked without raising his head.
     "His report."
     "But what is this?" He raised his head.
     "I don't know?"
     "Do you deny that you've recommended us a madman?"
     "He wasn't mad."
     "Was he in the war here?"
     "Yes."

The Chief leaned forward over the table, holding his temples in his hands. "It's some kind of post-traumatic stress disorder."

I felt a lump in my throat. The Chief was looking at me. He seemed so far away, as if we were separated by more than just space.

"Maybe it's a put-on," I said. "If he were totally bonkers he wouldn't have lasted so long—he wouldn't have made it to Baghdad."

"Did he send crap like this from the beginning?"

"He did," I admitted.

"Really?"

"I covered for him because I'd recommended him. I rewrote his pieces."

"You've really fucked up."

"He's playing some kind of game. I've studied these pieces of his for days. He wants to seem madder than he is. When he came to Zagreb the first time he showed me some of his writing. It was the same."

"PTSD prose," sighed Pero. "Now PTSD prose will become the issue of the day. Brilliant. We have to publish proof that he got back to us. But not this. Have you got anything that came for this issue?'

✉

From: Boris <boris@peg.hr>
To: Toni <toni@peg.hr>

Allegedly the Yanks have Saddam's DNA, we know how that works from detective soaps, the forensic experts work like maniacs, and this is better than Dynasty, there's oil. From a plane you can see the family's palace, and we can identify them by means of the Y

chromosome and the mitochondrial DNA, since a son's
chromosome is 99.9 per cent the same as his father's,
and if they find remains of the three corpses with the
same Y chromosome beneath the ruins of the palace
there's a high probability they'll be remains of Saddam
and his sons, and in order to be able to say which are
the remains of the sons and which are Saddam's the
experts will have to use a different method of analysis,
the one based on mitochondrial DNA, popularly called
the Gospel of Eve, because every person carries his
maternal mitochondrial DNA, so Saddam's sons have
to have the same mitochondrial DNA as their mother
Sajida, whom her son Uday ordered to be killed in year
2000 of the Common Era. Then, historically speaking
a little later, we set off toward the president's quarters,
where the asphalt is scorched at the intersections,
the lampposts have snapped like matchsticks and
the occasional corpse lies by the roadside, and you
can see a humongous building the color of sand. Two
soldiers from the 2nd Infantry Division lead us in,
there's no electricity in the big halls, massive pearl
chandeliers lie among the stuff on the floor, waiting for
the tradesmen to come and repair them, the soldiers
warn us not to go up to the first floor, which hasn't
been cleared of booby traps. Next to the palace is
the so-called Baghdad Miami, a building with several
domes, a garden, swimming pools with built-in bars,
now an American detachment is there, dusty soldiers
sitting around the swimming pools with their stale
water, among them a marine originally from Lika in
Croatia, who left ten years ago because he's from a
"mixed marriage," there was nowhere for him to go
other than America, and now he's an American. They
call him Pete, he said, he's as well as well can be, gets
Western wages, and he asked me how things were
back at home, and what sort of car I drive, for example,
and whether I knew an old school friend of his called
Karakaš who went on to become a journalist.

So we'll take Saddam's DNA and hunt around a bit and see if he's alive or dead. That's the main question, as usual. If you have dealings with someone, first check if they're alive or dead, and only then get in touch so you don't go getting worked up for no reason, like when I was standing by the swimming pool where my old man died, where he was taken away by a heart attack under the sun. I've chatted with him in my mind, I've raved with him, all the Arabic has been ringing in my head for years, so I returned to the place by the swimming pools where they were searching for the dictator's DNA, the DNA of his son Uday and the mitochondrial DNA of his mother Sajida, but like hell they're ever going to find anything, that's like searching in the sludge, and I'm sinking in this rot, in this Arabic, all these days, I'm going down here amidst the war, in this universal mess, in this soul of mine, in nothingness.

"We can't publish this," the Chief said.

I know that, I thought. I wouldn't have falsified these pieces if they'd been publishable. Now you can see how I felt.

"What the fuck am I supposed to do with this?" he said.

I looked at him with sympathy as if to say: this time it's not for me to decide.

Having seen the full depth of the problem, Pero fell silent. He leafed through our back issues with my texts and Boris's photos. "You know, I hate to admit it, but you really do a good job."

He glanced at me with what amounted to respect, like you regard a thief who can open any lock.

"It's nothing," I mumbled.

"When he comes back he'll be a star reporter after all this media hype," Pero said.

"Anything's possible."

"I've got an idea. It won't be in his interest to tell people that we didn't publish him, right? That would make him look like an ordinary loser, not a reporter the whole country was looking for. And if he doesn't come back, he won't be telling people either."

I must have been wearing a gloomy expression.

"Hey, I'm just thinking aloud. We have to keep all our options open," he admitted. "When you add it all up, nothing's stopping us from continuing. I mean, he does send the odd snippet of information. And you can beef it up, give it some normal conclusions and a normal tone."

"Hang on, you want me to keep pretending to be him?"

Pero nodded.

"For how long?"

"This really is the best option," Pero said. "Or have you got a better idea?"

If the charade continues, the others play along and I keep pretending I'm him, are they going to treat me *as* him in the end? Will everyone ultimately agree that's the best? Would I have to knock on Milka's door one day and say: "Mom, I'm back!"?

I needed to clear my head. I went down in the elevator and left the building. I thought of going for a walk—a long walk. I was on the sunny side of the street. Nothing special, just everything you'd expect: buildings, ads, cars, people, and offensive graffiti scribbled by Nazi-minded kids.

Walking along the four-lane avenue there, I thought of me and Sanja. It was a strange flash like remembering someone I knew long ago. For a second I saw us in a photo from one of her birthday parties.

I was pierced by a sudden and inexplicable sadness.

I ought to have done something with my life, I thought—I
ought to have done something instead of messing around and
botching things up. I was always just patching up my reality.
I didn't want to go back to the office and I was afraid to go
home. I imagined all the neighbors would stare at me. So I
thought now was the time to go and see the flat—the one
from the classifieds. It was high time. I had the number in my
mobile. I wanted to see the flat so badly, as if I was driven by a
superstitious urge and would be able to comprehend my fate
there.

I called the people. They were doing the place up or
something. Then I called Sanja and said, "We really ought to
go and look at that flat. We have to finally do it, you know."
I whispered it as if we were inmates and I was suggesting a
breakout. She was still sleeping. She asked if there was anything
in the papers about the play.

"No, I didn't see anything."

"I really can't now, I'm still sleeping," she said.

I don't know why, but I'd always thought there had to be a
modicum of telepathy in a relationship that would spring into
action when needed.

My whole life I'd secretly been waiting for a miracle. And
now it was high time for it to happen.

It was an attic flat, reasonably large, with quite a few angled
walls. I liked that: we could do all sorts of wild things with it
to make it look rebellious. Now everything was white, but we'd
add our own color scheme: yellow, red, orange, plus some crazy
pictures, and perhaps some stupid graffiti. That way we'd be
young and crazy again, rant and rave—that was the only thing
that could save us.

I paced from the living room into the kitchen, peered

through the window, went back to the living room, into
the kitchen, and had a look in the bathroom. I stood in the
hallway for a moment, then went into the bedroom and eyed
it up and down as if I was noting the dimensions. Then back
to the living room.

The owner and his son kept walking behind me, watching
me like the peasants in Van Gogh's *The Potato Eaters*. Big eyes.
I couldn't take in the flat properly with them behind me: I
was only pretending to be viewing it, and I didn't know what
I was seeing.

"Goood!" I said with a superior tone of voice, as if I was
some important inspector.

The owner and his son trundled around after me like cars
behind a little steam engine.

They wouldn't leave me alone.

"May I use the bathroom?" I asked schoolboyishly.

I stood in the bathroom and exhaled as if I was catching my
breath after a steep climb. I reflected for a minute but could
sense the two men on the other side of the door.

I flushed the toilet and came out.

And they watched me.

I looked at them.

The son glanced at his father to see what he thought
because he was even older and heavier.

I began to walk around again, admiring the views.

"Well?" said the father.

What now? I liked the flat. But had they just painted to
cover up a leak? Why the recent renovation? Should I pay the
deposit and get it over with?

A weakness comes over men at the very thought of having
to make a decision about buying something. That's the reason
they bring women with them when they go to buy clothing:
women will turn a shop upside down until they find what they

want. A man doesn't have the strength for that. He buys quickly, impulsively, wanting to hurry up and finish what he's started, just like sex. A woman is taught to turn things down, she's constantly saying no, even a promiscuous woman is constantly saying no, because if it wasn't like that everything would be different and no one would ever go to Thailand for sex. Men go all the way to Thailand, but for every woman Thailand is just around the corner, in every bar, every business and even every religious group, because there's nowhere she won't find a man to offer her sex. The world is one enormous brothel for women, but they pick and choose, they're after that extra quality and say "no" until they get it. That's why it pays to take them with you whenever you're buying something, especially a flat.

But Sanja wasn't here. I felt that if I hesitated too much I'd never buy the flat. She'd leave me, the flat would be gone, and everything would drift away. I wanted to do it before it was too late. The best thing would be for me to get out the damn deposit. I rummaged in my pocket, but I didn't have it with me.

As I meditated on my empty pocket the son turned on the TV. The song "We Are the Champions" came on.

The stage was full of stars, and Mandela was with them. Probably some kind of repeat.

We are the champions, we are the champions, the audience sang.

I looked around the flat again. I peered into all the corners, felt the walls, stared at the parquet, and turned the taps on and off. Father and son walked behind me. The silence stank of freshly whitewashed walls.

I asked why they were selling the place. They said they'd inherited it from an aunt who died.

"Did she die here? In the flat?" I asked.

The son stared at the floor, but the father said, "No, in a hospital."

"I have to consult with my girlfriend. We're getting married soon and we'll be buying together. I'd be happy to get out the money right now and pay the deposit, but I need her to come with me so she can have a look."

"Well, you've seen the apartment now, so feel free."

I went down the stairs, four stories without an elevator.

Out on the street I turned and looked once more: a fine old Austro-Hungarian building. The façade slightly dilapidated. Less than ten minutes' walk from the main square.

Perfect.

A Croatian reporter is missing in Iraq, the radio reported as I was driving back.

Later in the office, I found myself sitting at the computer in the role of the missing reporter. I had to write one of his pieces. It was almost as if he'd officially taken me over. I'd been working at being him for two hours already and I was still stuck on the first sentence. Back when I was falsifying things in my name—back when no one knew—it had worked. Like when you're masturbating somewhere: you can fantasize about all sorts of things as long as no one is watching you, and then you return from that fiction and the world is still the same. But this was different, it was a lie we'd agreed to. It was irrevocably becoming my world.

I made myself write, but my language started to flake and fall apart.

You have to. You have to! You want to take out that loan, stride boldly into the future, buy a nice shack and lounge around there in style. You have to, this isn't for fun, you have to. Your whole life is ahead of you, just as it always has been. I have to, I have to, I told myself.

Finally, I slapped it together. Another Boris report from

Iraq. It was muddled and not much different from Boris's style. If he had post-traumatic stress disorder, I wasn't far off it myself.

My bloody mobile kept ringing. Always unknown numbers. I put off answering. GEP's title page gave me no peace. When colleagues came into the office they gave me a sympathetic wave or hello, treating me as if they'd come to pay me a visit in the hospital.

I ordered a Vodka Red Bull at the little café by the staircase. Something had to give me a lift. It was just one o'clock in the afternoon, and I was losing the fight against sleep. I drank by myself. Charly and Silva hadn't come in yet. Still wrecked from the night before. No call from Markatović either, no word from Sanja. They were all still sleeping. Even the muvver of Niko Brkić who was s'posed to play in Nantes would be a welcome sign of life.

And then Dario appeared—just who I needed to make my day. He ordered a macchiato.

"How are things?" he asked.

"Fantastic, brilliant." I said.

"Did you get on to Rabar yesterday?" he said sarcastically. I said nothing.

"Are you for real? I haven't told anyone, but you go calling GEP, ask for Rabar, and then today this sabotage comes out. A bit strange, huh?"

I grabbed him by the collar and pushed him up against the wall. "Don't tell anyone about this, got it?"

His eyes bulged.

"D'you hear me? You're not going to tell anyone about this, or about Rabar," I growled, tightening my grip on his throat. "I could kill someone after all this shit!"

I let him go, and he stood there coughing. "I won't say a word," he spluttered, steadying himself. Then he shuffled toward the office.

The waitress was staring at me.

"He's forgotten his macchiato," I remarked.

I drank the Vodka Red Bull. Then my old ma rang. She was in shock too. How could it be, how was it possible, she just didn't understand. I heard her out. It seemed she was the focal point of everything: her phone kept ringing and people kept asking her questions. We were wrecking her nerves, she said, she'd end up in the psychiatric ward. Still, she cursed Milka and was on my side. Dad, on the other hand, offered to come if I needed help. He even came up with the idea of calling Milka and smoothing things out a bit so there wouldn't be any further complications.

He soon called me back. He'd phoned Milka, and she'd told him: "I'm going to hang up on you like your son did to me." He told me that my ma had then also called Milka, although the two of them weren't on speaking terms, and started swearing at her as soon as she answered the phone, so Milka couldn't give her a talking to. They exchanged salvos of insults, with my mother occupying the moral high ground: we'd tried to help Boris and find work for him, and she was treating us like dirt.

At that point my mother took the receiver and said I should always tell people that; she always started by saying that we found Boris a job because people understood that and then they were on our side. Everyone knows how hard it is to find work nowadays, and if someone's helped you, you can't go whining in the newspaper, because Iraq isn't any more dangerous than Bosnia was, and Boris was in Bosnia, so how can Milka claim he's inexperienced? Who sent him to Bosnia anyway? If you put it like that, clever people are on our side, my old ma told me. We had about thirty percent support, by her assessment. "So tell that to the journalists! I dunno who they think they are. We'll come when you need help. Call us," ma added, as if she was messaging from HQ to boost morale.

We'd closed ranks. I felt part of the family again. A combat unit: me, my old man, and ma. Even my sister rang. She was pregnant with her second child and living in Sinj, but she still made a point of getting in touch and asking if I needed help. She could knit socks for those of us in the trenches, engage in propaganda, and look after the wounded, I said. I shouldn't make light, she replied: she was there and was always on my side, whatever I did. I felt her support. The strength of the family—strength in unity! Like a little mafia. Only my family understood me. They knew who Milka was and who we were: who was the aggressor and who the victim. That's how it is when a local conflict escalates. Outsiders don't understand a fucking thing.

After all that, the office secretary called and told me to see the Chief. It was urgent, she said. Dario, I assumed, that little turd got up and went to Pero's office. His feet were up on his desk.

"Your old ones were better."

He was holding the latest issue of *Objective*.

"I'm a little unfocused," I said, taking a seat. "Didn't get much sleep last night."

He was still staring at me as if I was an exhibition piece.

"Could you get up for a minute, please," he said.

"Is this some kind of joke?"

"No, please, it's very important."

I stood up.

"Step back a bit, please, toward the door."

He took his feet off the table, got up and moved about, regarding me from different angles. He scrutinized the issue of *Objective* he was holding. "You know? You look a bit like the guy from Iraq."

"I hadn't noticed."

"It only just dawned on me now."

"What's dawned on you?" I asked weakly, standing near the door, wanting to turn and run away.

"Have you given me all the photos you have of him?"

"What's been published is all we have."

"We don't have a photo of him from Baghdad—and that's what we need," Pero said. "I thought of Photoshopping Baghdad into the background, but we can't do that with these photos we've already used. With your physical similarities it occurred to me that we could take a photo of you and sort out the background on the computer."

"You're not serious."

"It's good you didn't have a shave this morning. We're going to tan you a bit, stick on some shades, give you some headgear and field clothing—no one will know the difference."

"I can't do that," I protested.

"Hey, who started this shit?" The eternal question in the Balkans. "Find the nearest tanning salon and do maximum exposure."

I was stupefied. "Can't you find some disco bro to do that?"

"No, you and Tosho are going to do it. He'll photograph you and do Baghdad on the computer."

"Then why doesn't he just tan me on the computer too."

The Chief's tone became threatening. "You'll play along. You'll 'come back from Iraq' the day after tomorrow. You'll walk about the office and stroll about the city. We'll take your photo on the main square smack in front of the Ban Jelačić statue. Then let GEP try and prove you're missing in Iraq."

"Are you crazy?" I sputtered. "A tanning salon?"

"Do you realize we can sue you over this? For fraud! For damaging our reputation. For commercial damage. For endangering peoples' lives. The boss has been cursing and swearing at me on the phone all day! Are you aware of that?"

"No, I didn't . . ."

"But you act like you're some kind of prima donna! 'Oh deary me, I don't want to go to the tanning salon.' Go to the tanning salon."

Juliette Beauty Center: I entered as timidly as I did the first time I went to the chemist's to get condoms.

A tanned blonde and a tanned brunette—one of them was bound to be Juliette—were sitting and sorting lotions and creams. Tropical aromas and Eros Ramazzotti were in the air.

"I'd like to get tanned," I said.

"Setting?" asked the brunette. She's probably Juliette, I thought.

"Um, maximum?" I said, a little intimidated.

"What do you mean 'maximum'?"

"I don't know how much is allowed?" I asked, thinking of desert conditions. "I need to get a good tan like the sun's really given me a whack."

"Have you been for a tan before?"

"No, I haven't."

"The first time. What would the maximum be?" Juliette asked the blonde.

"Y'mean you really wanna full blast?" the blonde asked me.

"Well, yeah," I said.

"OK then. Put 'im on twenty-five minutes," the blonde suggested.

"Twenny-five?" Juliette asked the blonde. "Really?"

"How about fifteen?" I asked.

The blonde looked at me as if I was gutless, while Juliette seemed open to compromise. "OK then, twenty! How 'bout that? The sunbed's pretty strong. That oughta be enough for you."

She led me into the next room, opened the sarcophagus,

and explained that I just needed to pull it down when I was lying inside. And close my eyes.

"You've got two minutes to get undressed," she said.

A humming began as the solar motors started. Now they were finally going to launch me in this capsule far away from everything. I'd shoot out naked into space. I felt warmth, a stream of air, and through my closed eyelids I saw a pinkish glow. Points of pink light glittered. I felt I was melting and turning into a slimy liquid like the guy in *Terminator 2*.

Then pictures came to me—parts of pictures. Mixed with parts of other pictures. It was like a chaotic little film. I was with Sanja in the theater. A camera flashed and didn't go off anymore. Then afterward, but still in the theater, we were looking up into the sky—there was no ceiling or roof, and I appeared as a parachutist, coming down out of the sky, laughing. Then the camera walked about the office—a very wobbly camera. Sanja came into the office and glided through it on one leg like a ballerina. Darkness. Applause.

There was a knocking and ordinary white light again.

"Still alive?" asked Juliette. Dark-haired Juliette, that center of beauty, looked down at me as I lay there naked, dark-skinned and hot. "You OK? We've been waiting, but you didn't come out."

For a moment I thought of pulling her inside the sarcophagus so we'd be in that universe together.

"I had a hard night."

"All right," she lowered the lid so she wouldn't see me anymore, "time to get dressed."

I opened the tanning bed again. The old rebel rises from the dead. I looked in the mirror. I looked a bit like James Brown. Ai feel gud, ta-na-na-na-na. I wiggled my hips in front of the mirror, and my dick waved in a semi-erection. They say tanning is a mood-lifter. See, it's true. Besides, I'd finally got a bit of shut-eye.

I had half an hour until the photo session and wanted to cool down but was paranoid about going to a bar where I'd be recognized, or even worse, not recognized at all. When my beer came, I called Markatović.

"Have you finally woken up?" I asked.

"Yes," he said, "and you?"

"A lot of shit's been going down."

I was going to tell him some of it, but he started sobbing. He'd finally read Dijana's fourteen-page letter. "Am I really so bad?"

"I've asked myself the same question," I said.

"All the stuff she wrote, it all sounds true. I'll prove to her that it's not true if only she gives me another chance. I'm always able to explain everything when she gives me a chance."

"She'll give you a chance," I said, and it occurred to me that everyone gets to lament before me. This is a country of lamenters—you can't get your turn.

"I don't know why I can't cope with marriage. I mean, I did cope with it—out of seven days I coped with six. But it just keeps going, there's no day off."

I almost laughed. Still, I tried to console him. "Come on, don't take it so hard."

"There are wonderful moments too. Like, let's say, when the kids were born," and he burst into sobs again. "It was a miracle. Do you understand?"

"I understand."

"I was so happy and couldn't take my eyes off them—the

first fortnight, the first month, the first six months. But it just keeps going, it all just keeps going."

"Yeah, OK." I was waiting for him to finish this shit.

"She says I've been avoiding them, that she's lonely. She says I should devote myself to her again so she knows I love her."

"And so you should!"

"But I can't do all that I should do," and more tears flowed.

"Are you still high?"

"I can't. I can't love her anymore! How can she expect that of me? But the letter says I have to love her. "

"I don't know. I mean, you don't have to—she's your wife."

"I have to, I have to. I used to love her voluntarily, but now I have to. That's the difference. It's not of my volition."

"How do you mean it isn't? You married her," I said.

"Well, yes. And now I have no choice anymore! You understand?"

The conversation puttered out. Markatović said farewell as if he was going to curl up and die.

A little later Pero the Chief rang.

"You don't have to go and get photographed."

I knew it. The tanning had just been his way of having revenge.

"Well, at least I got a tan at the company's expense," I quipped.

"It's too risky. Besides, we have to go on TV tonight. The *Up to Date* team called—they're dedicating the whole program to it."

"Look, it's best I don't go on TV."

"We'll go together."

"Listen, man, I'm tanned like a glamour puss. No one's going to take me seriously. Who believes a tanned guy?"

"We have to tell our side of the story," said Pero.

"No one will understand," I pleaded.

"They'll brief us, and we'll make our case point by point. There'll be guests as well: Boris's mother will be down in the regional studio. You'll have to face up to her. We'll have to patch things up a bit."

Milka? Via videolink?

"No, no way, I can't. I'm unfocused, I haven't slept, and I'm at the end of my tether. Plus—I'm tanned!"

"Take it easy. The lawyer and PR will brief us. We'll work out every word. We only need to challenge that he disappeared, that's all. Surely the two of us can deal with an old biddy."

"I can't, I really can't. I've given my all."

He cursed and hung up.

There had just been an excellent review on Radio 101. Hadn't I heard it? They praised her sky-high. She'd wanted to record it on cassette but mucked it up in her rush, Sanja reported.

"I'm in the car on my way home but I haven't turned on the radio. Have you not heard anything else?" I asked.

"I heard what I heard—and you didn't," she said.

"That's not what I meant, but never mind. Have you just got up now?"

"Come on, don't phone while you're driving. See you soon."

"Oh, by the way—I'm tanned."

"And I'm in heat," she purred and hung up.

It was bulk waste collection day in the neighborhood. Everyone was clearing out their cellars, and a jumble of oddments rose in front of the building: old mattresses, washing machines, ravaged furniture, stoves, and unidentifiable sponges. I looked at the scene and felt like sitting down on the armchair with the missing armrest or lying down on the sagging greenish couch—and being taken away with all the junk.

Romany lads dressed in tracksuits and secondhand uniforms from the war were hanging around, sifting through the stuff and calling out to each other. "Djemo, come and give us a hand with this."

As I was backing in beside the heap, Djemo in his half-sporting, half-military gear showed me how much room I had. Then he signaled me to stop.

Djemo probably mistook me for one of his people, tanned as I was, and when I said "thanks" in Croatian he looked at me a little surprised. Then a girl walking past in a miniskirt and high heels caught his attention. Djemo whistled quietly, long and drawn-out like wind across the plain. He then launched into song: *Here comes the sun, little darling . . .*

How I envied him.

"Come on, Djemo, stop fucking around," yelled his friends, who were loading a pickup. He went over to them along a green and shining tree-lined path.

A lady came out of the building carrying a battered picture of a shipwreck in a massive frame. She looked at me askance.

As I was getting out of the elevator, Charly called and launched straight into a confused spiel. "Know what? You're right."

He's just got up too, I thought. Man, am I the only one around here who works?

"What are you talking about?" I said.

I'd already rung the doorbell for Sanja to open.

"She's not bad at all."

"Who?"

"Ela. Who else? She slept here and made breakfast. She's gone now. I can tell you, it was a really pleasant morning. And the night kinda wasn't bad either. You're right, if she lost a bit of weight she'd be cool."

While he was talking, Sanja opened up for me in her
dressing gown, with a cigarette in her mouth. She acted as if I
was a stranger. Then she casually turned, went to the couch, sat
down, pulled up one leg and opened me a view of her pussy.

"Yes, yes. Look, I have to go now."

"Good you came along, mister," she said, as cold as Sharon
Stone. "My husband's not at home."

I gave up the idea of telling her about my day. I just stood
and watched her smoke. That was our sex-theater. We liked to
play raunchy scenes.

"You sure have got a bit of color," she said, fighting back a
giggle.

"I'm coming in from the desert."

"Oh, it's very hot here too," she said, stroking her finely
shaved pubes.

I told her to put on the costume from the play.

"So you're the photographer who said he'd be coming?"

She went into the bedroom and came back dressed. White
miniskirt, push-up bra, and little white boots. Cute little slut.
She strutted in front of me like a catwalk model. Then she
went to the hi-fi and upped the music. Massive Attack.

I grabbed her bum under the miniskirt. "You've forgotten
your panties."

"You've got the wrong impression of me, mister," she replied
in that feigned, uppity voice.

I had an acute erection. We kissed. She nibbled my lip a
bit. I moistened my finger and gently pressed her clitoris. I
crouched down. She parted the folds with her fingers and
bared her clitoris, inviting me in.

"Gawd, you're a photographer with a sense for detail," she
said in the timbre of a lady who admired artists.

"Uh-huh," I confirmed with a mumble.

She moaned. Her legs began to tremble.

She pulled back. "Fuck me!"

I stood up. She shifted to the couch and got on all fours. I smacked her on the bottom.

"Are you a singer?"

"Uh-huh," she moaned.

"A proper singer or a little stage slut?"

"I don't know," she admitted bashfully.

"Sing a bit and screw around a bit?"

"Yes."

I slid into her.

"Like that?"

"Yes."

"Where do they screw you?"

"Grab my ass."

I gripped her firmly, raised her a bit and lowered her onto my cock.

"Are you filming all this, mister?" she asked after we'd both been panting for a while.

"Uh-huh."

"Will I look good in it?"

"A bit vulgar," I said.

"I'm so, I'm so ashamed," she grunted.

"Why are you ashamed if you're a little bitch?" I raised and lowered her faster and faster, breathless, incandescent, emitting the mania of that day.

"I'm. I'm a good girl," she gasped and then howled, jolting, as her orgasm overcame her. "Come on, just a bit more," she begged.

I thrust into her hard a few more times. Afterward I collapsed beside her. I kissed her shoulder and closed my eyes. She stroked my hair. We just lay there. I didn't want to fall asleep, so I opened my eyes every now and again.

"That was a good fuck," she said. "You like the costume?"

I put a cushion under my head as I nodded. "If I drop off, don't let me sleep longer than an hour. Don't turn down the music. It's just right."

"I'm going to the theater now. I'll set the alarm clock for you."

"OK."

"By the way, that review is a must. It's on the web," she mentioned.

"I'll read it. Did you know they've caught on to the business with the guy in Iraq?"

"No, you're kidding. What happened?"

"I'll tell you later. I'm too tired now."

Up to Date was a political and cultural talk show with universal appeal and a studio audience. The host was a skinny woman with a shrill voice who could cut off every guest with that vocal cleaver, so there was no straying from the topic: the Croatian reporter missing in Iraq. It was to be the final showdown between me and Milka, on the TV battlefield, like in an epic folk song.

I was frightened, but they called me a hundred times on my mobile, threatening me to make sure I attended. In the end the big boss himself called me. By nature he was perhaps even more perilous than Milka. I tried to convince him that it would be better for someone else to go in my stead; but no, he fiercely insisted that I was the one. He told me that he would do everything in his power to make my life worse if I didn't go. So he ordered me to go and tell my tale and make a stand against her with arguments; she couldn't make accusations without evidence, he said, whoever's mother she was.

So there I was finally—*Up to Date* due to begin any minute. I was sitting in the studio, my nose powdered, in the black blazer I wear to premieres and funerals and which people in

my village recognize me by. Beside me sat Pero the Chief in a
Versace suit and glasses; he was there to stiffen my spine and
protect the firm as the second line of defense in case my first
line was breached, or I fled. With us sat GEP's running dog,
the little guy who penned the article (they called him Gruica),
as well as two neutral commentators who'd have to make up
their minds whose side they were on: the president of the
Croatian journalists' association, and a bearded sociologist,
who'd written some book. And there, arriving with some delay,
was a government representative, a chargé d'affaires from the
Foreign Ministry. The Chief told me that if Boris had really
disappeared the government would now officially have to
search for him, so that would no longer be my job.

That was the first piece of good news for me in a long
while. And so we sat there, confidently manning our defensive
position. The lawyer said we were squeaky clean in legal
terms because we hadn't forced anyone to go to Iraq; Boris
had signed an employment contract like everyone else. Our
mistake—which we were only to concede if they cornered us—
might have been that we didn't raise the alarm soon enough;
in other words, if they really cornered us, our mistake would
be mine. But here I had a counter-argument, namely that Boris
could still get in touch: the deadline hadn't yet expired, and
all the fuss was based on speculation, although we too were
worried. Our PR lady assessed that we were in a relatively good
position; we just had to avoid engaging in spats with Milka
because she was a mother and that would not go down well.
We all agreed that Milka should be given a wide berth, and our
PR damsel continued that we had to be sympathetic with his
mother, smooth over the misunderstanding, promise her hills
and valleys, offer help and legal protection for our employee's
family so as to win it over to our side. She also told us to come
out straight away and say that GEP wanted to destroy us, so

that later everything would be interpreted in that vein, and change the conversation to that topic—say what the foes had done to us so far because they hated a respectable paper like ours; in that way we could do a little advertising as well.

But alas, as soon as I saw Milka in the regional studio via videolink I knew that the jig was up. She was sitting there in berserker mode; her head thrust forward like a dog straining at its chain. It was clear that she couldn't sit still in the camera's glare: she squinted and could hardly wait to start. She'd prepared her tirade without solicitor or PR consultant, her head was full, and you could tell she was bursting to vent her fury.

As soon as the host had greeted the viewers and briefly outlined the problem, she swiftly gave the floor to the missing journalist's mother, naturally, and Milka struck at me via videolink. She addressed me as "wee Toni." This confused the host, who requested Milka not to call me that, irrespective of the situation, to which Milka replied that she'd always called me that. From there our whole plan went pear-shaped.

"I've known 'im since 'e was knee-high to a grasshopper," Milka said. "Of course I can speak to my snotty-nosed nephew like that."

"Just a minute—you mean to say you're related?"

"We sure are," Milka replied.

The host glanced at me and couldn't contain a taunting laugh. "Is that true? You sent your own cousin to Iraq?"

At that point everything went to pieces.

The president of the journalists' association laughed loudly.

The system of nepotism had had a stranglehold on the country for a whole decade; war had created openings for the hill tribes to enter the system; warriors and outlaws infiltrated it, brought along their relatives, created networks, and built up para-structures. Our urbane intelligentsia had been combating the hill tribes for a decade already, mocking their clannish culture and kin-and-kith morality because they were a millstone around our necks, a mafia in government. We'd never have a modern state until we civilized them. They had to realize that the world was not about relatives. They had to refuse the call of the tribe and become individuals.

"Let's be perfectly clear," the host said. "This journalist you employed—who then disappeared—he's your own cousin?"

I'd long pretended to have become civilized, emancipating myself from the call of the tribe, but this was it: now they'd seen through me. There I was on prime-time television.

The Chief looked at me, bewildered. Everything we'd discussed in the briefing fell through.

"He is my cousin," I said, "but he knows Arabic."

It was no use. My words sounded ridiculous even to me.

I must have phased out because for a while I didn't even follow what was said; little pictures went round and round inside my head and I saw the flat I'd been to see that morning. I knew the show was now on TV there and everywhere, it was going all round the world via satellite, and, I don't know why, I thought of Charly watching me on the screen, gaping at me with a bottle of locally-grown olive oil in his hand and cooking his slow food that he wouldn't invite me to eat.

After a while someone in the studio audience asked to be able to speak. They passed him the microphone.

None other than Icho Kamera.

"I 'appen to know Milka, an' all. I know the situation an' I can say it ain't all black and white, like. Milka oughta realize that they found 'im work, after all 'e was unemployed an' wanted a job. An' this guy, the journalist, found work for 'is cousin. I reckon that deserves a bit'a respect!"

Bloody hell, he spoke as if he'd been briefed by my old ma.

A short round of applause from the studio audience. The host then gave the floor to the sociologist with the beard, who proceeded to deep-end the audience into the phenomenon of tribal relations, of regional differences that were extra-institutional. They hindered the functioning of institutions by creating a parallel system. That was our particular problem, he stressed. The strongest states were those that had destroyed tribal relations and weakened the extended family. "The stronger the family, the weaker the government," he concluded.

The host called on me to comment. I said I agreed with the gentleman from the audience, and with the sociologist.

"Only you don't get on with your aunt?" she asked with irony.

"No, I can't get on with her."

After that they switched back to Milka in the regional studio. First she replied to Icho Kamera, saying that everyone knew he was crazy, and as well as slamming me she also came down on the sociologist for what he'd said against the family. Basically, Milka had been poorly briefed and seemed to have forgotten to cry and talk touchingly about Boris, so in the viewers' telephone voting she received a much smaller percentage of support than expected. We had thirty percent, just like my old ma said.

After the show, everyone instinctively edged away from me; only Icho Kamera came up in his somber old jumper. "I see ya're gettin' popular, kid. I remember you."

"I'm gettin' anti-popular."

"'T's all the same: popular, anti-popular."

"You're in Zagreb pretty often."

"I got me sons to look after the crop," he said. "I sell a bit at the market 'ere, an' I also go to things like this. Livin' down south is borin' for me—this 'ere is the center of things. I mean, what can ya do down there?"

I listened to him with a tad of admiration. Icho Kamera talked like young people who don't want to squander their life in a backwater where nothing was going on. He wanted to be in the flow of things. In the focus. If he could speak English he'd definitely be off to New York. If he wasn't such a pleb, no one would notice he was mad, I thought.

Pero the Chief came up to us. First he spoke to Icho and shook his hand. "I think we ought to thank you. Your support means a lot to us."

"As a man in the street I had to say somethin'," Icho Kamera said.

Then the Chief turned toward me. "The boss called me just now. You're fired."

"Fucking hell."

"That ain't right," Icho Kamera said.

"I get the impression he's going to sue you as well."

"Ooh, that ain't nice," Icho Kamera commented as we headed for the bar. "To sack someone like that—to jus' toss 'em out."

"It'll raise the motivation of the others," I said.

"That's why I never wanted to be employed. Just farmin' and a bit'a TV—I'm me own boss!"

While I was drinking with Icho in the bar, Sanja called me. She had three minutes before she needed to be back on stage. She'd seen the beginning of the show and a bit near the end.

"After rain comes shine," she said awkwardly.

"Get on with your stuff, don't worry about it anymore," I said.

Afterward I went to Limited. Everyone looked. Markatović arrived to console me with the story that he was doing even worse: Dijana was gone and the bank's shares were still falling.

"I've heard reliable information that the Germans are giving up. They're offering the bank to the government for one kuna," he said. "But, on the positive side, Dolina rang today and he's angry."

Dolina had apparently also seen me on TV. He was convinced I'd tarnish his image and demanded that Markatović, who hadn't started on Dolina's campaign yet, find someone else.

"He says you're compromised," Markatović said, imitating Dolina to try and sound snappy.

I didn't have the strength to smile, so Markatović stared at me hypnotically. "That pretender of yours is going to come back alive and well."

"That's the drugs talking," I said.

"No, really: it's always like this when it's to do with someone else. With these shares I have, if someone else had them I could predict without error. He'll come back, really—we can bet on it."

"Let's not. You've gambled enough already."

Then Markatović started talking about his old man, who'd turned to drink soon after entering his son's employ. "He probably feels humiliated. He's spiteful all the time. In his head, I probably represent capitalism. It's the same with your guy. They both feel we're on the other side: we're part of the system, in their eyes, and they need someone to blame. Since they don't have a political agenda they take it out on us via the family."

We boozed till closing and then went back to his place. If nothing else, Markatović finally had the apartment to himself.

I sent Sanja a message that I was going to Markatović's and that I might sleep there. I sort of wanted to avoid her, as if I felt ashamed in front of her.

We sat there in the mortgaged flat. It really was a super apartment. I took the remote and turned up the volume a bit when I saw the Rolling Stones on TV. It was a press conference prior to a concert in Munich.

"Look at them," Markatović said, hunched slightly and staring at the screen with open mouth and bloodshot eyes.

"What's the secret of your timelessness?" journalists asked them. Keith Richards, still looking like he'd grown up too quickly, answered, "That's a secret," and roared with laughter.

"Just look at him, will ya?" Markatović said.

"He must be sixty already," I said.

"He drinks the most expensive wines, models line up to get into bed with him, and he still manages to be a rebel," Markatović marveled. "Man, he'd go mad if they put him in a down-market hotel."

"Yes, when he's rebellious," I said, and sniffed a line of coke from the chess board.

"Two hundred thousand people were there, and tomorrow all of them will be going to work," Markatović said.

"Of course, they work."

"Every day they repress what they admire about Richards. Every single day they repress everything they admire."

"Of course."

"It started way back with Jesus."

"Do you also get a strange feeling when you mention a big word like 'Jesus' or 'revolution,' like a weariness comes over you?"

"I don't know."

We fell silent.

Footage of people who'd been to the Munich concert was now being shown. They claimed the Stones were the same as before. Indestructible.

Markatović and I were destroyed. We'd grown up in strange Eastern European systems and placed too much hope in rock'n'roll. We lived with that therapy for years and thrived on hope. Just let things settle a bit, we thought, and we'd all be like Keith Richards.

"Hillary Clinton isn't bad either," I suggested.

"Just think of little Eminem," Markatović said. "I saw a documentary about him. The guy grew up in a trailer park and was really fucked up. He rapped around in a few sheds, but then he recorded an album, sold a few million copies, and got rich! And what's he going to do on the next album? Y'know, he's gotta be rebellious and have that face for another fifty years."

"Yeah, he'll have to get pretty drugged up so they don't see through him."

"First you're fucked because you're fucked up, and then you're fucked because you're not fucked up. That's the life of a rebel for you."

"There's no going forward and no going back."

"You're not allowed to sort yourself out," Markatović said.

"Why would you want to sort yourself out?"

"I don't know, that's just the way things go. You sort yourself out, and along come the problems."

We laughed.

The Stones played on, indestructible. Markatović snorted more coke.

"Did you really want to get yourself sorted out?" I asked. "Or..."

"Or what?"

I shrugged.

"Hey, I got married, bought an apartment, had kids— When did you ever do any of that?"

"OK, so you're more forward-looking," I conceded. "And you stayed a rebel."

"Right. Even Iggy Pop goes to the gym. Red Hot Chili Peppers go to the gym. Not me."

"I used to go before I had a bathroom, to use the showers."

Markatović puffed up his chest proudly, making no attempt to hide his beer belly.

Who knows what it means to be rebellious nowadays.

"Now I'll be going without a bathroom too," he said, referring to the steep drop in RIJB-R-A shares.

It might sound nasty, but I felt better being with Markatović. The whole problem with Boris didn't seem so terrible to him. He was knee-deep in shit himself. I assured Markatović that everything would be OK and that he'd get out of it in the end. I told him it was good that he was waiting because the government would intervene sooner or later and sort things out. He just needed to be patient a bit longer.

"It's different when it's your own dough that's inside and when it's about saving your own neck," he sighed. "Then you're not so sure of things."

I don't know how things got to this point of me having to reassure him all the time. I mean, he'd been expecting that of me from the beginning, so why was he now opposing so vehemently? Now I had to be even more convincing. That's how it works. Someone gives you a role and you do your best to hold onto it. You forget how things began.

"Come on, man, Rijeka will be going up tomorrow. The government has to intervene. It's as clear as daylight if only you look without fear."

"OK then, you've consoled me," Markatović said.

I snorted another rail of coke.

"Life is a song," I said, breathing deeply through my nose. "The song creates feelings. Words in your mouth take you over."

DAY FIVE

I woke up on Markatović's couch; my mouth was dry, my legs were stiff, and my head hurt like hell. The TV was still on and two psychologists were talking with children about good and evil.

"Bad is when one kid builds a sand castle and another comes and knocks it down," a boy said.

The coffee table resembled a waste dump. We'd polished off the hard stuff by the looks of it. I leaned my elbows on my knees, put my head in my hands, and tried to be wise after the battle by accessing the damaged parts of my memory. A little bird hopped along the balcony railing. It didn't sing. The children went on about good and evil, they understood that in the morning. On the evening program everything looked more complicated.

I got up and inspected Markatović's shelves, opened the

drawers, and peered into decorative bowls full of knicknacks until I found a tablet and took it.

I looked at my mobile: 11:21.

A text message from Sanja: "Had a roaring night out? Take it easy. Call me when you wake up. xoxo"

I called her to say that everything was OK except that my head hurt.

"Come on, take a tablet or two and make some coffee. Have you got a lot of work today?"

"I got the sack."

"You're kidding."

"No. It's as real as it gets."

"When?"

"Last night after the broadcast."

"Why didn't you tell me?" she asked, as if I'd broken some rule.

"You were at the play. It's all the same whether I told you last night or today."

"What are you going to do now?"

"I don't know, I'll see. I don't know. Sorry."

"Don't apologize."

I felt I'd let her down. There were probably a few expectations of me somewhere in the cosmos of our relationship. I think it was taken for granted that I'd move up in the world and not go down. "Sorry."

"Oh no, no," she said. "I'm sorry. I don't know, I've just got to the theater. Go home now. Don't keep drinking."

"What would I do at home?"

"Don't keep drinking now, OK?"

"I'll be OK. Don't worry."

I made myself some Turkish coffee, went out onto the balcony and sat in the wicker chair. It was a nice day, I looked at the greenery and the city far below. Fresh air. A little blue tram skimmed along down below. People were driving places. I had no idea what to do. The day lay spread out before me.

Should I keep drinking? Or go home? Into town? For a walk? Should I go to the zoo, perhaps? Take Markatović and go to see the elephants?

I opened Markatović's bedroom door a crack. He was lying diagonally in the double bed. He blinked his eyes.

"Sorry, just you sleep," I said and closed the door.

My mobile rang. Unknown number. It was a journalist. She asked if she'd reached me.

"I hope so," I said.

She wanted me to comment. She began by launching into long-winded, treacherous flattery, which I interrupted.

"I'm to blame," I confessed, and hung up.

Markatović opened the door a little and stuck out his head. I didn't know why he was being so cautious. A remnant of his married life, I supposed.

"I'm not going to throw anything at you," I said.

He came in. "Fucking hell."

He dragged himself to the coffee table and slumped into a leather armchair. He sipped the coffee and we spoke in incomplete sentences. We were listless and disgusted by our own hangovers. He recalled a nightmarish dream: Dijana and the twins, each at the wheel of a steamroller, had been pursuing him across an incredibly large parking lot in front of a shopping center he wanted to reach the entrance of, but it kept receding.

"Congratulations," I said. "I dreamed I was puttering around on the internet, there were some passwords—and I don't remember the rest."

"You didn't dream that."

"How do you know?"

"You were on the internet last night. You placed an order on the stock market. Don't you remember?"

"No!"

"You bought Rijeka. I was telling you not to. Don't you remember?"

I turned on the computer. I looked at my mobile—12:40. The stock exchange started at ten. It depended on the price I'd offered; perhaps the order didn't go through.

"If this happened it's your fault," I said.

"My fault? I kept telling you not to. You were so adamant I assumed you had some insider information." I went to my brokerage firm's site. He was right. I'd bought 3,000 shares in a failed bank. Since the market had opened RIJB-R-A had already fallen to 43.30 kunas. I'd lost 21,600 kunas while sleeping on that shitty old couch.

"I only claimed everything with Rijeka would be OK to make you feel better. I do such a good job I start believing my own bullshit. Bloody fucking coke!"

I swore and cursed for a full ten minutes, pacing furiously from wall to wall. Markatović, still sleepy, sat in the armchair watching me.

"This is your fault," I carped.

"Come off it! I told you last night . . ."

"Why the fuck did you make me say everything would be OK?" I moaned. "Why did I have to run into you in this stupid life?"

"Bloody hell, Dijana said that to me all the time!" The veins on his neck strained and his voice screeched bitterly. "A friend comes over, sleeps here, gets up the next morning and takes over where she left off. I'll throw you all out of my life, head over fucking heels. Got it?"

I left that unlovely, odious house amidst its accursed greenery and went around to the foul-smelling parking lot.

There was my car.

I got in and stared at the wall I was parked in front of, wanting to drive right through it.

The city perspired in the midday sun. Trying to be European, it wore the most modern rags and expensive labels. Sunglasses and street cafés sought to invoke the flair of Milan and Vienna. It was the brainchild of girls from marketing agencies, urbane press officers, and unemployed spokeswomen, different permutations of Markatović, literature editors who were starting to forget classics, and screenwriters of domestic sitcoms. It was full of future plans and plots.

I went in search of a daily paper. GEP's *Daily News* was selling well. I had to go to three different kiosks before I could get a copy. AL-QAEDA SILENT ABOUT THE FATE OF CROATIAN REPORTER. It sported a photo of Boris and the sub-heading: "Boris Gale, whose employers concealed his disappearance, was last seen in Baghdad six days ago."

How on earth did al-Qaeda get into this?

Standing at the kiosk, I opened page two of *The Daily News*. Down in the corner next to the main article there was a box with the heading NEPOTISM. It reported that Boris had been sent to Iraq by PEG's editor, who was also his cousin, "which speaks volumes about the way that news corporation functions." They didn't mention me by name, but more as a metaphor for perversion. I'd obviously had my five minutes of fame. Milka received better treatment: a photo and a little tribute to her grit.

I took a seat at a café on the main square where old ladies with showy coiffures pretended to be remnants of the Hapsburg Empire. I didn't want to go into a bar or café where I might meet someone I knew. I put on my shades. From now on I'd camouflage myself between the old ladies and the relics of former regimes.

I read the paper to find out why al-Qaeda was silent about the fate of the Croatian reporter. Obviously they'd come up with the title first, so they sent inquiries about Boris to certain websites allegedly linked to al-Qaeda. No reply came, and if you looked at it that way al-Qaeda was indeed silent.

And what of Boris? What if cuz latched onto the heroin produced by the Afghan Taliban? What if he were ultimately found having overdosed in a Baghdad bathroom?

I tried not to think about that. It was best to be silent for the time being, like al-Qaeda, and read the paper and sip my coffee inconspicuously in the street café, dissolving into the masses. But copies of the paper were on every table. AL-QAEDA SILENT ABOUT THE FATE OF CROATIAN REPORTER, they screamed. As if we were so important for al Qaeda to target! Yes, we wanted to be a part of the global spectacle!

Hard to believe I'd created this whole ruckus. It was as clear as daylight to me that my story was impossible to understand. It'd been full of idiocy and madness from the beginning—or even before that. But I went along with the game. For years, day in day out, that balderdash had been building up in the language I used to form my thoughts and opinions. I had my role. It bothered me when I spoke, it bothered me when I thought, it bothered me that I existed.

An old lady from the next table watched me attentively and blinked like a lizard about to lash out with its tongue. She's sure to have watched TV last night and now she thinks she's seen me somewhere. You could tell she was racking her memory, which, fortunately, was overloaded. All the same, I was terrified for a moment that she might recognize me. But who was I? My image had collapsed in one single day. I was surprised I could represent myself at all.

I called Sanja. I wanted her to reassure me that I was still me and to keep me in one piece.

"We could go and see the flat!" she said with enthusiasm.

"I really don't know if it's the right moment now." I felt it was too early to mention that I'd sunk all my money into shares.

"We can talk about it at home. Come home, will you?"

"I can't get a loan now."

"Come on," she said in a trusting tone of voice, "maybe I could get one. They might be giving me a permanent contract. Possibly starting as early as next month."

"Yeah, great."

"Aren't you happy?"

"Sure, I'm happy," I said. "There's just so much going on. I can't keep my mind on everything."

"Yes," she agreed, pensively. "Haven't you seen the review in today's *Daily News*?"

"Was there something?"

"They really heaped praise on me."

"I'll have a look."

"There's something about Boris too," she added.

"I've just bought a *Daily News* now but haven't got round to reading it yet."

"Maybe don't read it. Better take the classifieds and think about positive things."

She was trying hard to cheer me up. I felt guilty. She should have said: Why did I have to meet you? And: People are disgusted by you and laugh with derision. And: You're not even a villain, but a media caricature. I imagined people at coffee tables making jokes at my expense. Those voices were bound to reach her too. She hadn't shown any signs of being influenced, but the more considerate she was, the greater my guilt became.

I browsed through *The Daily News* again and found the culture section. There was a lengthy article about *Daughter Courage and Her Children* under the title STRIPTEASE PUNK. The critic speculated on the meaning of the play and went on at length about the role of rock music in the East and West. Ingo had set the plot with the rock group on a "Western front," so this theme kept coming up. Rock assumed a paradoxical position from the very beginning in the conflicts of East and West, the critic wrote. Although it burst onto the scene in the West in the '60s as a rebellion against the system—often with an openly leftist bent—it was to become a weapon of the West against the Communist East. Rock embodied the culture of freedom and represented the essence of the West—at least that's how it was always perceived by young generations in the East. So rock definitely played a role in the collapse of Communism. It may seem strange to someone in America, for example, that Frank Zappa fans in the Lithuanian capital Vilnius had erected a 4.2-meter monument to their idol in 1995; it was made by the sculptor Konstantinas Bogdanas, who'd produced a serious sculpture of Lenin for the 400th anniversary of the University of Vilnius in 1979.

The critic, however, was not sure whether Ingo's play referred to the role of rock in the Cold War or in today's East-West conflicts. So was Ingo perhaps caricaturing Huntington's thesis on the "clash of civilizations"? Or perhaps both conflicts at the same time? The critic praised the play for its complexity and multiple layers of meaning, citing that Ingo—because he "didn't seem particularly well-informed"—probably didn't have our ex-Yugoslav East-West conflicts in mind, where cultural opposites such as rock vs folk, urban vs rural, Western vs Balkan, and Croatian vs Serbian belonged to the politico-cultural arsenal to be used whenever needed, in war or peace.

I skipped part of the piece, down to where I saw Sanja's name: "This former member of the group Zero performed with great instinct, creating a powerfully feminine figure with fascinating charisma."

My mobile rang. Silva.

"I heard you got the sack," she said. "Sorry to hear that."

"Not the first and not the last. Globalization goes hand in hand with particular processes. Everything is interconnected these days. Someone makes a mess in Iraq, and I have to carry the can here."

"Good you can joke about it."

"What else can I do?"

I surprised myself by the way I was talking to Silva. It was if all my despondency had disappeared. It occurred to me that with Sanja I couldn't any more act the cool freak; it was like I was obliged to be depressed because I'd disappointed her, while I owed Silva nothing.

"Did you know that Pero got the sack too?"

"You're kidding."

"Nope. This morning. The boss blew his top. You did both look pretty dumb last night."

I laughed.

"Don't laugh. That's tragic, not funny," Silva continued. "Now your cousin on the other hand—that's funny."

"It is tragic—not funny."

"Sorry, but I died laughing when he turned out to be your cousin. What do you think's up with him?"

"How should I know? I just hope people will stop asking me about him one day."

"I get you."

"Now the whole country is worried about him. The guy is sooo significant that he needed me to find him a job."

"But he has disappeared."

"If he'd disappeared in Solin or some other dump here he could rot there and no one would bat an eyelid."

"No one knows what's up with the guy."

"The concern for him is one hundred percent to do with where he disappeared—Iraq. The center of the universe right now. It's got fuck all to do with real concern for him as an individual."

"No need to get angry. We'll see what happens." She hung up.

I continued the conversation in my head: it's a lie when you say you care. It's just what's on TV today: a film about a Croatian reporter who disappears in Iraq. You feel part of it and identify with the hero. Not with the anti-hero.

The old lady who'd been watching me got up, came over, and stood right in front of me. Some old ladies are most impertinent, if you consider that their death is just around the corner.

"Yes?"

"Are you the young 'un who disappeared in Iraq?"

"No, and I'm not the other guy either."

"Oh dear," she shook her head. "We were so excited. We thought we'd found you."

I entered the flat with the newspaper under my arm. Everything was just as before, yet it seemed I was coming back from a long time away. On the coffee table, the classifieds were still there with flats circled. Two glasses, the ashtray, an empty pizza box. I got myself a glass of water and sat on the armchair in front of the TV. The silent screen stared at me dully as if waiting for me to do something.

Noises came from outside and filled the room's heavy, motionless air. The lighter clicked; flame appeared. I inhaled.

I looked at all our things. Everything seemed too full; there was no more space. Out in the street the sounds of traffic rose in volume. Cranes filled the view out the window. Congestion there too.

Sanja and I had once been free here, outside of everything, with our kisses and long dreamy gazes into each others' eyes, envisioning future days. But now the walls had been breached and run-of-the-millism flowed in from everywhere and nowhere: the stench of society.

For the first time since dropping out of Drama I felt I had to write. I had to commit all this to writing. Perhaps it'd help me to step back from things. I'd be able to stay sane and see everything in perspective; I'd arrange everything in an order that made sense.

I had a flashback to me and Markatović drinking beer in the canteen, back when it seemed all paths were blocked and the gloom was oppressive and suffocating. Back then we already knew about all the horrors that people have just started writing about today. Evil had touched and tainted us. That torments us even today, I thought: we have no trust and no faith in this reality, this peace, these people, or ourselves.

It was already dusk; I didn't turn on the light.

Later the phone rang, the landline. "Guess who this is?"

"No idea," I said and hung up.

Much later I heard the lock turn. Sanja opened the door and turned on the light.

"I'm here," I said.

A whole roll of newspapers was jutting out of her bag.

"Hey," she looked at me rather frightened, "why are you sitting in the dark?"

"I had a headache, so I turned off the light."

"Is it better now?"

"No."

"Want me to turn it off again?"

"It's up to you."

She turned on the reading lamp and switched off the ceiling light.

"You shouldn't smoke if you've got a headache," she said. "What are you drinking? Is that rakija?"

"Water."

She crouched beside me and stroked my face. "Tell me what's wrong."

"I'm not well."

"Why are you looking at me like that?"

"My head hurts."

"What happened?"

I thought deeply about that. All sorts of things had happened, and nothing was left. I wanted to talk like that, without endless, futile explaining. That standard language wearied me with its questions and answers.

"You can't just sit there in silence—say something!" She started to sob like a smacked child.

I shut my eyes. "Don't cry, please. It's just that my head hurts."

She calmed down and searched for tablets in the drawers. She handed me one. "Here, take this."

I swallowed it.

"Today I bought shares in Rijeka Bank. I placed the order last night over the internet, I don't think I knew what I was doing. When I woke up it was all over."

"You bought what? Say that again slowly."

"The dough I had—it's all in the shares now."

"In what shares?"

"Rijeka Bank," I repeated.

"But that's crazy. That bank has collapsed."

"That's just speculation."

"Jesus, Toni, what's going to happen to you?"

"I wanted to see how far I could stretch my luck," I told her almost enthusiastically. "Free myself of everything in one fell swoop. There was no plan, it just happened, like a natural disaster."

We were silent for a few moments, and then she said, "You know, maybe you should talk to someone."

"We are talking."

"I'm not a psychologist."

"Do you mean a psychiatrist?"

"I can't tell how all this has affected you. I don't understand."

"Good. OK. Point taken. Can you chill out a bit now? You don't need to ask me anything."

"Why not?"

"Because there are some things you just don't get."

"Why are you saying this?"

"Look, you're not the right person for me to talk to about some things."

"Why are you being so nasty? What are you doing to us?"

PART TWO

Sanja was lying on the bed in the room, facing the wall.

"I'll come for the rest in a few days," I said from the door. And then I started sobbing.

"Where are you going to go?"

"I've found something temporary."

"You can't go now, like this," she sobbed.

"So you mean I shouldn't go?"

Three days earlier she'd told me that we couldn't go on like this. And burst into tears.

"It's so horrible, it's all so horrible."

I went up to her, sat on the edge of the bed, and stroked her hair.

"My love," I said as quietly as I could, "my great love."

Regret burned me from the future, from the time we wouldn't be together: that future nostalgia, an awareness of the oblivion that would blanket everything.

"Don't forget me." I kissed her hair and whispered, "I'm going now."

She didn't turn around.

I got up and took my old rucksack and suitcase. I looked at her from the door, her shoulders were shaking. My gaze roamed the flat one more time, I nodded goodbye to everything and left.

Nine in the evening, it felt like coming out of a darkened cinema. The story is over and you're outside again. I stood in front of the building and put my bags on the ground. I took off my sunglasses. The neighbors were out walking their dogs. I hailed a taxi, gave the address, and said nothing more.

I paid the driver and entered the small building. I went up the stairs with my bags and stood on the second-floor landing at the door with someone else's surname written on it. I opened up the bedsitter I'd rented two days earlier, just to tide me over. It smelled like rancid walnuts. I put down my bags in the middle of the room and just stood there, then pointlessly raised my arms as if I was about to say something.

Here the film should have ended. It was high time for the credits.

I turned on the radio. Chi-ki-chi-kaa—the old jingle of Radio 101. Youth Radio. At least that's what they used to call it back when I listened to it alone in my room soon after arriving in the city, with that great emptiness in front of me. I didn't have a TV set back then. I took the ashtray out of my suitcase and lit a cigarette.

A small '80s shelf along the wall. Kitchen the color of milky coffee. A brown fold-out couch. Traces of pictures on the walls. A window with a view of a car mechanic's workshop, judging by the cars in the lot the mechanic specialized in old Opels. A round table that I now sat at—like at an aborted meeting.

This was Tosho's neighborhood. Everyone here was known by the name of Joe. I ought to go into the nearest bar and say, "Hi Joe," to check if the trick worked. But I didn't feel like going there.

I called Tosho to tell him we were now neighbors. It rang somewhere in the vicinity. He didn't answer; he probably didn't have my new number. I thought of texting him that it was me.

Me.

Chi-ki-chi-kaa. News on the radio. Casualties in Iraq.

It wasn't over.

After my television appearance, there were various theories about Boris's fate: that he'd died, that the Americans had killed him during a disturbance, that he'd fallen prey to the Baghdad gangs that attacked foreigners, that he'd been kidnapped and was being held by Islamists, and even that he'd gone over to the Islamists, because the public had somehow got hold of his original reports and allegedly discovered anti-American positions. Psychiatrists specializing in post-traumatic stress disorder joined in the debate and detected a paranoia in his sentences, as well as a shattered sense of his own worth, suicidal tendencies, a schizoid imagination, and a feeling of impairment and guilt. There also seemed to be confused traces of the recent ex-Yugoslav wars as well as the war in Iraq, because war was war and for him they fused together and became one.

Fifteen days after I got the sack, GEP's *Daily News* started publishing Boris's original reports in installments. I don't know who handed Boris's original reports to GEP. *Objective* wrote that it was me. I, for my part, suspected Pero—his revenge on both PEG and me.

Now it all was out: *Objective* had been publishing phony reports from Iraq. Dario wrote a piece in defense of PEG, laying out his discoveries about my role in GEP's plan to monopolize the newspaper market. He confirmed that I'd threatened to kill him if he revealed I'd been in touch with Rabar and that I had doubtless been working against my own newspaper the whole time. Maybe, he wrote, even Boris's supposed disappearance had been a sham. Only time would tell. I consoled myself with this last bit: if Boris's disappearance was part of the plan, then at least I wasn't a murderer.

As it continued, and while Sanja and I were still together, I pined away in the flat with the blinds down. She urged me to see a shrink and said she would pay for it, but I refused.

It was one literary columnist's belief that Boris's reports were actually very original works of literary worth, which I'd interfered with and disfigured; publishers later came along and expressed an interest in issuing them as a book. Editors hadn't figured out who was whom because they rang me to inquire about the rights. I referred them to Milka.

And just when all that madness, like every rejected hot topic, was starting to sink into oblivion, Milka began calling me again. I didn't answer.

Then my mother called me: Boris had called Milka from Baghdad.

"Why didn't he get in touch, the stupid asshole?"

"Milka said 'e'd kinda got depressed and couldn'a be in touch with anyone, an' now 'e was takin' American tablets, she canny explain it 'erself."

"American tablets?"

"Milka said he got depressed an' lost his mobile, conpewter and all, or else they stole it from 'im; 'e dunno 'imself."

"American tablets," I repeated. The story went on: Boris had been saved by an Englishman who took him in and looked after him, and that he was bedridden. But now he was on the mend. He'd be staying in Iraq and working for some British TV channel, Milka said.

"She told me, 'e'll be scoutin' out things they wanna film. Out in the field, like. I forget what they call it—oh yeah, field producer. 'E goes round and asks about everythin', 'cause he knows Arabic," my old ma said.

"I know! All because he knows Arabic."

"Well, it cert'nly seems to 'ave been of use to 'im," she continued. "You know, I really let Milka 'ave it in the end! I told 'er: 'All right, now your son's got work. An' 'e's bound to get good pay, too, what with workin' for the British an' all. But my son lost 'is job because of your hullabaloo.' And you know what she said? 'So what! I'd like to see you in my position. Boris could'a died there in Iraq,' she said. Well, you know 'er, she's not gonna apologize. She really rubbed me the wrong way. But I told 'er: now she should 'ave the gumption to apologize, like, in the newspapers and on telly. That's 'ow she attacked, so that's 'ow she should . . ."

"Stop talking about her. It's driving me mad."

"Don't you go mad too, sonny. It's good that 'e's alive an' you don't 'ave 'im on yer conscience. But I'm not givin' your number to no one no more. Not that anyone's askin'. "

I put down the receiver. He's gotten in touch—it's all over, I repeated to myself, like I was announcing it to someone approaching from afar. But my words resounded emptily, like the voice from a loudspeaker in a large, forgotten hall. All I heard was the thudding of my heart. If only he'd been killed it'd all make more sense. Should I go to Baghdad and kill him? Everything would look more logical that way.

"But Boris is alive, after all, and everything could've been a lot worse," Sanja said, trying to believe that everything could be like it used to.

I just needed to return to the game, find a new job, and be who I was before. I just needed to assume my old face, light up a fag like Clint Eastwood and ride into a new film.

When she started being silent with me I asked her what was gnawing at her, but she wasn't able to say. She couldn't talk about that with me anymore. She waved her hands in frustration, complained about other things, and her voice had a tired, dead-endish ring. She said she was tense and took tablets to help her sleep. And then I started being silent with her. It seemed she'd had enough of my problems.

Jobs, flats, expectations, status, successes, the public, relatives, invoices . . . That whole construction was founded on love; everything else built up on top of it until love gave way. That was love's rebellion, I guess.

Today I tell everyone: we didn't get on anymore. But I don't know in what way we weren't getting on. It's just that an image that had once held us together had fallen apart.

She was now in a league of big-timers, all those characters were courting her and I had to compete with them.

There's something humiliating in the abrupt transformation in a change of status. There's something cruel in it because it looks like you're not yourself but more of a social construct— it's a nasty message that says what you are doesn't depend on you. I know it well.

"Are you cheating on me?" I had asked one evening when she came back from the theater later than usual.

"We just stayed back for drinks."

I asked her the same question again.

"What's got into you? And no, I'm not cheating on you."

"Do you still love me?"
"You could've asked nicely."
"You just need to say yes or no."
"Yes, dammit, I love you!"
"Good. I want to be sure of that."

In the beginning, it'd been a pleasure to appear in public with
an eye-catcher of a girlfriend; you enjoy that, her good looks
are your pride. But now, with her growing reputation, I was
starting to feel like a minder. The cretins stared at her as if they
had nothing better to do than to test and provoke me. They
looked at her, and I at them, and we sized each other up. That
tedious game kept repeating itself. I couldn't enjoy a bloody
drink in peace.

In the Balkans you get wrinkles early from the eternal habit
of sizing each other up. That mask was driving me mad. It was
fortunate that no one ever beat me up in front of her. I was
paranoid about that, I did push-ups and lifted weights every
day. At one stage my shoulder began to hurt. I took painkillers.
I went to the doctor and he said the pain was coming from my
spine, but I kept on training and taking pills. I went around
with my face, my spine, and my muscles. She enjoyed herself,
while I had to drink to kill the stress. I thought of getting
myself a pistol so I could stop the training.

My back really was giving me a hard time. I didn't feel like
going out anywhere. I tried to find excuses. I criticized the
aggressive social situation, cursed the war that had led to such
a macho society in the long term, imprecated the media and
their fascination with violence, railed about hardly being able
to breathe because of the packs of frustrated dudes who hated
the women they couldn't get.

We went out around town less and less, so we had to visit

people at home. And we—or rather she—had lots of new friends who invited us to their places for dinner. They were mostly elite sorts, well informed, and they knew about my professional debacle.

Finding work turned out to be impossible. With my fucked-up reputation I could only start from scratch. Should I accept an inferior job and completely destroy every illusion about myself? It was better to be a domestic philosopher than an errand boy for someone else, right? That's why I preferred to stay at home and watch programs glorifying the nation, drink beer, smoke, and complain about capitalism, which has been truly weird and wonderful in Eastern Europe.

We have capitalists here who've never engaged in what Marx called the "original accumulation of capital," I said, watching TV. Instead of accumulation, they only did a redistribution of capital. The capital already existed, it's just that its owner was suddenly gone. The capital was social, and the society it belonged to disappeared. The people disappeared from the economy and went off to war, all of them; they thought only about the border because they saw the state as a border to be defended. The state was then empty inside, there was no one around, and the capital roamed around looking for an owner. You only needed to lie in wait in the deep, dark forest of the law and waylay it like Hansel and Gretel or Little Red Riding Hood.

I made excuses. Told Sanja I refused to work in a capitalism that was made during the war from melted-down socialism. That was wartime magic, a magic full of dead souls. *Dead Souls*, Gogol, *The Inspector-General* and other plays, I said. You can't work in it or even exist in it without being cursed by dead souls—the souls of dead proletarians. Here even generals became capitalists. How could you have losses at the front yet profit behind the lines?

"You watch too much TV and get too worked up," Sanja would tell me. "You think you're participating, but you might as well be watching things from Space Station Mir. Then at least you'd realize how far away you are."

"But I'm here."

"Where?"

"Here! On the edge of ruin here at the edge of Europe—the very brink of disaster. Can't you see it?"

"Toni, stop."

"Without politics we'd die of boredom, especially us unemployed. What would we talk about if the political system functioned?"

She didn't reply anymore.

Thinking about ourselves is the greatest horror in entertainment society, I pointed out, so if there was no "politainment" we'd have to become a different kind of society—one which reflected on itself and its emptiness and realized that we lack real, human-scale politics. Then perhaps we'd disintegrate. Groups and factions would fall apart from too much thinking and everyone would start thinking for themselves. But would that be good for the nation? No, we have to stay united. We have to be thinking about the same thing at the same time.

In front of the TV I felt like a real man, immersing himself in the political programs of the season. If I was a stereotypical girl I'd be shouting at Oprah and following the travails of Hollywood marriages. That'd be healthier, after all. But instead I watched TV, drank beer, and smoked. One way or another, our fantasy is the most important.

"You were right," I told Sanja. "Boris was right, too. He didn't falsify his existence, and I have to give him credit for that. He was a remnant of something real, he came from down south and knocked me off my chair and out of my world—a world I thought was mine. Really, it's stupid to lie that we're standing on solid ground. Now I'm outside, nowhere, floating in a limbo beyond lies; everything is clear to me now, but that doesn't mean I can make sense of it; I'm just talking, like he talked, it's as if he's infected me with it, so now I can't control the sense of what I'm saying, I just speak," I told her as I watched TV, drank beer, and smoked.

"You remind me of my dad," she said. "You just sit in front of the TV and get disappointed with everything."

"Maybe I'll protest out on the street."

"With who? Who do you have left?"

That was how I wasted our last days together.

I was sitting alone in that run-down bedsit, without a TV, when Markatović called. "Have you heard? They've suspended!"

"What?"

"The shares in Rijeka Bank. The state agency for financial supervision has suspended trading until further notice. They just announced it now."

"Are they allowed to do that?"

"To prevent manipulation, they say. The Germans have finally left. Trading in the shares will be suspended until it's decided whether to save the bank or send it into receivership."

They assured us that global capital would save us here in Eastern Europe and that we had to attract it like a new lover, break down the barriers, deregulate the labor market, and reduce welfare expenditure. Capital needed air to breathe so it'd feel comfortable. A lot was done to make capital feel welcomed, but in the end it made off.

Now I was borrowing dough from Markatović. I don't know whom he borrowed from.

One day I was waiting for Markatović. He wanted to discuss a business matter with me, over a beer in his bedsitter. Dijana had long since returned with the children. When she came back, Markatović was happy at first. But recently he rented a place near mine "until things got sorted out," as he put it. He intended to sell the big apartment and buy two smaller ones if he managed to reach an agreement with Dijana.

The bars with cigars had become too expensive for him, so he was going to collect me near an ice cream parlor on Gajeva Street. Then Silva called, which surprised me since no one from the paper had rung me for a long time.

"Listen, sorry, I just thought of you now. I'm at the hospital in the emergency room. My son's here with a very high temperature. They don't know what he's got."

"Can I do anything to help?"

"Have you noticed the game?" she asked.

"Which game?"

"'It Takes Two to Tango,'" she said. She explained that she worked on the side producing games and sweepstakes for *Today*. GEP's daily paper was full of things like that, so PEG had to counteract in *Today*. One of the games that had recently got off the ground was "It Takes Two to Tango."

"I really haven't noticed."

"You must have—it runs to a whole page. Part of the game is a competition for the best true love story. I came up with that idea."

I stared at an oil stain on the road.

"Are you with me?" she asked.

"I'm with you."

"But few stories come in, and they're not romantic enough."

"Not romantic enough?"

"That's right. So if you want to help, could you perhaps write one—by tomorrow morning?"

"You want me to write a romantic true love story?"

"Otherwise I'll have to write it."

"So now you're treating me like a renowned counterfeiter."

"No, no. Who cares? They're just stupid letters from readers. Their love stories. No one can check whether they're genuine or not. I'll pay you cash in hand. Otherwise I'll lose my side job."

"I wouldn't know how to make that up."

"Of course you do. It's pulp. Soupy genre stuff, cheap romance. You know: *te quiero, te amo, te* this, *te* that. It's always the same. Look at mine and copy." She spoke quickly. I imagined her standing near the entrance to the emergency room with her mobile, smoking neurotically.

"Come on, please. It's ten to fifteen sentences. I won't manage to do it, I have to stay here."

I spotted Markatović's Volvo coming up the street and started waving like a drowning man. He stopped; I opened the door, slumped into the seat like a sack of potatoes and nodded to him.

"Will you write it then?" Silva asked.

"All right."

"Thanks so much, Toni."

"I just hope your little guy gets better."

"What's up?" Markatović looked at me askance.

"Silva's son is in the hospital."

"Is it serious?"

"They don't know."

We drove toward our new neighborhood. Stopped at a traffic light I stared at a blue building under construction.

A lot of buildings like that were going up, the shares of construction firms were rocketing and people flocked to the stock market. It seemed everyone was on the winning end apart from us.

"How can they make such ugly blue monoliths? Are there no building regulations?" I said.

"There are much more important things that are unregulated, and you're worrying about aesthetics? How are you going for money?"

"Broke as usual."

"What are you up to then?"

"Some writing."

"You too?" he said disappointedly. "I need you to pay me back some of the money I gave you. My loans have dried up. I gave my old man the sack."

It all happened very quickly after parking the car: as Markatović was getting out, two shapes emerged from the semi-darkness of the parking lot and grabbed him. There was one on my side who grabbed me from behind, but I managed to slip from his grasp before he could tighten his grip. I pulled back, and he struck me with something on the shoulder. I saw Markatović being beaten, and my huge attacker came at me again.

I ran behind a car. The guy didn't know which direction to come at me from. Other parked cars blocked my view of Markatović but I saw the gorillas kicking him as he lay on the ground. Behind me was a little park, where a neighborhood gang liked to hang out.

Like a flash of lightning I started yelling, "Joe! Hey Joe! Help!"

The guy who was chasing me stopped and glanced around.

A Joe appeared out of the shadows of the park.

"Help, Joe, help!"

Then Joe was joined by three or four more Joes.

The gorillas who'd attacked us weren't taking any chances; they ran off to a black BMW that was idling with its lights off, got in, and quickly slipped away.

Markatović was a mess. His lip was burst and bleeding, his face red, and one eye half shut. He held his ribs and could hardly breathe.

"Who were they?" the Joes asked.

"No idea," I confessed.

I called an ambulance. One of the Joes asked, "You fr'm the block here?"

"I'm not here all the time, but you probably know my friend Tosho."

He nodded conspiratorially as if he remembered me now.

"You sure saved us," I said. "I owe you a round when I see you next."

"Microregionalists," Markatović moaned from below.

One of them laughed for a second. They thought he was delirious. Only now did I notice that Markatović was missing one of his front teeth.

"They lost the elections," Markatović groaned, "but I made the most out of them."

I rode to the hospital in the ambulance.

"Are you in debt to Dolina?" I asked.

"They count every damn kuna."

At the hospital, before being wheeled in by the medics, Markatović gasped, "You try doing business in Croatia."

"Sorry?" the medic asked.

Markatović waved to me sentimentally, as if we'd never see each other again. The doors closed behind him, and I gazed about, disoriented. I was probably in shock too. I couldn't get "microregionalists" out of my head.

Then I noticed a blonde sleeping on a chair in the hall. She was holding her handbag on her lap with both hands and her head was drooping to the side: Silva.

I sat down next to her and stayed there and felt safe for some time. It would have been a pity to wake her. Her skin was pale and revealed her exhaustion.

Smoking was prohibited there, so after a while I got up. At the exit I texted her: "They're sewing Markatović up. I'm going home to write the love story."

At my bedsit I opened a beer, sat down at the table, and started leafing through an old copy of *Today*, looking for "It Takes Two to Tango."

I sat there for a long time, wondering what to write. What could I say? A man and a woman loved each other but their love was eroded by external circumstances, the world of work, social pressures, and the system none of us could escape?

The genre of romance doesn't acknowledge love that fails like this. It looks at the system aloofly and pretends to be above it. But I knew that genre lies.

I read yesterday's love story, by a Ružica Veić from Biograd, it said. Ružica worked as an au pair in Rio de Janeiro, where she fell passionately in love, only to return to Croatia in the end with her Brazilian beau.

So that was the scheme: a girl goes away to an attractive destination that evokes romance, falls in love there, and then returns home—because it wouldn't be politically correct for a story to promote emigration?

The story in Saturday's issue was almost the same, except that Ljerka Mršić from Osijek was an archaeologist, and the guy a rich Neapolitan, who, as she discovered by pure chance, happened to have Croatian roots.

I started writing:

It began in Mexico, where 25-year-old Milka Radičić from

Vrbovec went to work as an au pair. She'd been in a relationship with Borna who promised to wait for her and marry her when she returned. But in Mexico Milka's life was turned upside down . . .

My mobile tore me away from the story. It was Silva; she'd woken up in the waiting room and got my message. Her son was better—they'd got his temperature to come down, and they'd sewed up Markatović's lip, although they wanted to keep him for another few days because he appeared to have two broken ribs.

"I'll visit him tomorrow," I said.

She asked how the love story was going.

"I'm looking at yours and copying."

"That's the best way."

I got back to writing: *When she arrived in Mexico at the property of Alex Castillo, whose children she was to mind, Milka was surprised to find that it lay at the foot of a mountain whose peak was wreathed in smoke. Alex's younger brother, Eduardo, explained to her that they were beneath the volcano Popocatépetl. Everyone in his family always had a suitcase packed with basic essentials ready under their beds. Every Castillo, practically from birth, kept a travel-ready suitcase, which in turn reflected on their family's character and attitude about life, Eduardo said. Although no Castillo had ever needed to go away, they were always prepared to leave everything at the drop of a hat and set off into the unknown. "Such is life under the volcano," Eduardo told Milka.*

Milka took to Eduardo at first glance. And he to her. She was the first au pair who hadn't been frightened by Popocatépetl. Eduardo realized straight away that Croatia was a land of brave women. Soon love flamed up between him and Milka. But six months later Milka had to return to Croatia. She and Eduardo said goodbye beneath Popocatépetl, thinking they'd never see each other again. Just then, she almost wished the volcano would erupt and Eduardo would get his suitcase.

She felt pangs of guilt for her thoughts because that would be
a catastrophe for Eduardo's family, and her desire for him was so
strong that she feared it might really happen. On her homeward
journey she prayed to God that it wouldn't. She thought of
the worst scenario: of the volcano erupting and Eduardo not
managing to flee. It was with these thoughts that she arrived
home in Croatia only to find out that, in her absence, Borna
had started going with Lana, who, to make matters worse, was
also Milka's cousin. Poor Milka, no one understood her in those
difficult moments. People added insult to injury by telling her she
shouldn't have gone away to Mexico in the first place.

A week later, Eduardo called and said he was taking his
suitcase and coming to Croatia. In fear, Milka asked him if the
volcano had erupted, but that wasn't the reason. Eduardo said he
was coming because of the love in his heart, and Milka broke into
tears of relief and joy.

Around noon Silva called me. She was satisfied.

"Do you think it sounds authentic?" I asked.

"It sounds like a love story," she said.

She told me she would help me earn some money with
stories like that, at least until I found myself something else. She
could place such things in *Violeta*, PEG's women's magazine.
These stories figured prominently in that publication and were
signed with foreign, female names because readers didn't like
romance authors with domestic names—they didn't sound
elegant enough.

"Plus," she added, "no one would know it's you."

Soon after we met up for a beer in a secluded bar full
of mirrors. She brought my money, and told me, with the
flavor of that staffer's frustration I'd already forgotten, about
Charly, who'd been made editor in chief after Pero got

canned. "He's not chasing after me anymore," Silva said and involuntarily glanced at herself in the mirror. Dario had also ascended the ladder: he now followed Charly like a shadow, thereby displacing Secretary, who was pretty exhausted with party field work, plus his cholesterol had gone through the roof, and they could just about pension him off. The big boss, I knew, had become president of the Croatian Tennis Association.

More stories as we drank till closing time, and when the waiters asked us to leave I said, "My place? We could get a bit more booze."

"Is that what you think?"

"I don't think."

We laughed and gadded down the road. We ended up in bed. After sex she fell asleep, and I lay beside her on the fold-out couch. She woke up an hour and a half later—the first rays of light found their way in through the blinds—and she saw me sitting at the table with a beer.

"Are you OK?" she asked.

"Yeah, I just can't sleep."

"Just give me a moment," she said, searching for her bra.

"No no, please, you should sleep."

"I have to go home."

I didn't say anything. I thought I should stop her so she'd stay, but I was hardly capable of conversation. She got dressed in the half-light. Then she came up to me, bent over a little and looked me in the eyes.

"Hang in there."

"I'm fine."

"She's still on your mind, I can tell."

"It's got nothing to do with that."

"In any case, it's got nothing to do with me," she said, gathering her things from the table. "I'm cool. I've had so much shit, you wouldn't believe it. I'm resilient. I'm just telling you, for your sake. You have to get that story out of your head as if it never existed. Believe me, I know firsthand."

I thought how good it'd be if I loved her.

"You're probably right," I said. "Want me to make you coffee?"

She agreed to stay a while longer.

"Silva, I admire you so much," I told her as she sipped her coffee.

The wrinkles around her eyes danced in a smile of irony. "Don't be so direct."

"They've lifted it!" Markatović yelled over the phone.

He'd woken me up.

"Turn on your computer. Check the shares, they're moving again." His ribs had healed admirably. His bottom lip was still a bit thick in the middle but it kind of suited him, and he'd had a crown put on his front tooth.

I did as he told me and finally I saw the ticker working. RIJB-R-A. Right at the start it'd gone up eight percent.

"This could be my rescue."

"It'll get even better. It has to. There's still some way to go to my price, but it'll make it. It has to, it'll saunter its way up!"

"I'm sure it will." That impulse to be heartening was automatic, just like it had been in the past.

We'd known for some time that the situation with the bank had to be resolved because the government had taken over the majority share and bailed out the debts. The incident was no cause for jubilation, but the Rijeka region heaved a sigh of relief, as did Markatović and I. We'd just been waiting for them to lift the ban on trading so we could recoup the money we'd invested—back when we were other people.

Now things came full circle.

"I only want to get my money back—that's my target. When I make it to zero, I'm getting out," Markatović vowed.

"You'll make it to zero, take it easy."

"If I make it to zero—you'll make a packet, fuck a duck."

"We'll see," I said. I didn't want to take the wind out of his sails, but I had no intention of waiting till the shares reached his price. I was dead-set: I didn't want to get into that game. I remembered that drunken, coke-ridden night.

"Keep me posted, will ya? I have a meeting and can't watch," Markatović said.

I stayed at the computer. The stock market and all its numbers kept changing, and I watched the RIJB-R-A transactions. The sale price kept rising.

Just a bit longer and I'd exit that game.

The shopping center at the edge of the neighborhood was no different from any other. They all looked like small medieval towns—a castle and several narrow streets.

Here you finally had the right to stare emptily. Some people went to yoga or meditation to reach out into emptiness; I came here. I walked around slowly, peered at the shelves, touched a few things, and stared into nothingness. There were people here too, but it felt as if there weren't.

Finding a cart at the entrance, which resembled a triumphal arch, someone patted me on the shoulder and I heard a female voice: "Hey!"

Sanja.

She raised her dark glasses. I'd probably looked apprehensive, because her face was apologetic.

We held perfectly still for a moment, as if we didn't know what to do with our bodies. Then we kissed each other on the cheeks, not getting too close. I stepped back from that familiar scent of her perfume.

"Where did you come from?" I asked.

"Oh, you know." She looked as if she was both glad and uncomfortable to see me. "So how are you doing?"

"OK. And you?"

"OK."

I got the impression she didn't want to say things were great so it wouldn't seem she was doing wonderfully without me. But that's how she looked—great.

"You look different," she said in a gentle voice, with an insecure smile.

She shouldn't have said that, I felt. I've got over that persona. It can't be reconstructed.

"It feels strange seeing you," I said.

"You know, I'm in a hurry," she said.

"Sure, ok." I started to turn away when she stopped me.

"You can come with me if you want."

She checked her phone. She had a strange new hairdo.

"Where to?"

"You'll think it's crazy. But look over there, at checkout number six. Do you see?"

I nodded.

"At 4:00 we're going to do something. Me and a few girls. You can join in. It'll only take about twenty seconds."

Twenty seconds? What girls? She seemed to be alone.

"What are you going to do?"

"We're going to shout, 'We are the cham-pi-gnons,'" she laughed.

Once, this probably would have made sense to me.

"We are the champions? Like in the song?"

She saw that I didn't understand, and I saw a trace of anxiety that she tried to cover up with a smile. I could read every grimace and gesture on her face; that was bound to be mutual.

"Champignons!" she said

"As in the mushroom? Why?"

"There's no sense in it. None at all."

We were standing slightly stiff, taking care not to make any false movement from the past.

"I'm just shopping."

"I just thought. Never mind," she said and looked at the time again. "I'm off!"

She vanished among the shoppers. I pushed the cart and set off behind her to see what would happen. She was close to checkout number six when she turned around and saw me. She winked.

Girls converged from various directions. Ela was among them. Doc and Jerman.

I let go of the cart.

It came suddenly and thunderously loud. "WE ARE THE CHAM-PI-GNONS!"

People were staring. I joined in and we yelled a second time: "WE ARE THE CHAM-PI-GNONS!"

Suddenly the others dispersed. I also got a move on. I pushed my cart as if nothing had happened.

My heart was beating hard. I looked back toward checkout number six. We'd escaped them.

One checkout girl was showing another where we'd been standing.

There was nothing where we'd been except for the shiny floor.

I felt a strange flux of happiness. We'd simply disappeared.